CHRIS LOWRY

Zombie Blues Highway Battlefield Z

Copyright © 2017 by Chris Lowry

All rights reserved. No part of this publication may be reproduced, stored or transmitted in any form or by any means, electronic, mechanical, photocopying, recording, scanning, or otherwise without written permission from the publisher. It is illegal to copy this book, post it to a website, or distribute it by any other means without permission.

First edition

*This book was professionally typeset on Reedsy.
Find out more at reedsy.com*

Contents

1	CHAPTER ONE	1
2	CHAPTER TWO	8
3	CHAPTER THREE	14
4	CHAPTER FOUR	18
5	CHAPTER FIVE	24
6	CHAPTER SIX	28
7	CHAPTER SEVEN	41
8	CHAPTER EIGHT	49
9	CHAPTER NINE	53
10	CHAPTER TEN	57
11	CHAPTER ELEVEN	61
12	CHAPTER TWELVE	64
13	CHAPTER THIRTEEN	68
14	CHAPTER FOURTEEN	71
15	CHAPTER FIFTEEN	79
16	CHAPTER SIXTEEN	83
17	CHAPTER SEVENTEEN	89
18	CHAPTER EIGHTEEN	94
19	CHAPTER NINETEEN	97
20	CHAPTER TWENTY	108
21	CHAPTER TWENTY-ONE	111
22	CHAPTER TWENTY-TWO	115
23	CHAPTER TWENTY-THREE	118
24	CHAPTER TWENTY-FOUR	122

25	CHAPTER TWENTY-FIVE	128
26	CHAPTER TWENTY-SIX	131
ABOUT THE AUTHOR:		136

CHAPTER ONE

I blamed the motorcycle. I would blame the kid, and if I was a little more advanced in the brain department, I'd blame myself, but it was totally and completely the motorcycle's fault.

A dirt bike has a distinct sound when locked in at fifty miles an hour. The road rolls under you in a blur, and if you're on a highway that once aspired to be an interstate running from Alabama all the way up to Memphis, there is no traffic to contend with.

It's a deadly combination that caught better bikers than me and turned them into road rash warriors.

I left Fort Jasper at dawn, a good-bye kiss and wave to my second family before pushing the bike outside of the gate and kick starting it as the sun lifted over the trees. I had two jerry cans strapped to the back of the bike with fuel, a backpack with food, a rifle, pistol and ammunition all with me on my steel horse. I couldn't help but think cowboy thoughts as I navigated the five miles to I-22 that ran from Birmingham into Memphis. My hope was the low traveled corridor would be free of cars, and Z, passing through and around mostly small towns in the rural hinterlands of Mississippi all the way up to the large city.

It was.

I locked in at fifty miles an hour over the gently rolling asphalt, close enough to the line in the middle that I could cut across the median if needed, or work my way to the shoulder on the right.

I had it all planned in my head, and at fifty it would only take four hours to reach Memphis, find a way to cross the bridge, and then two hours or three to Little Rock.

In the head is the wrong place to be after the world war with Z.

It's where the memories stay, and random snippets of cowboy movies played out thanks to my monkey mind's thought bubble about steel horses, which led to a Bon Jovi song playing over and over until it was usurped by Toby Keith. Then titles of movies, and bits of dialogue.

"Reap the whirlwind."

"I'll be your huckleberry."

"I did bad things boss, and I don't like to think on them."

Which made me miss the actors I once loved, and hoped some of them made it. Kevin Costner took the mantle of cowboy movies and did a damn fine job, and I listened to an interview with him once where he talked about how hard he worked his ranch. He could have survived if he prepped it.

I watched his movies with my son, trying to instill in him a love of Westerns. I wasn't sure it worked, but I planned to ask him.

That thought sent me on playing out different plans on how

to find them, how the reunion would go, what excuses I would make for being late.

Which carried me to the outskirts of Southaven Mississippi, a suburb just before the state line and Memphis city limits.

I pulled off to pour gas into the tank, shook out some of the dead legs caused by vibration and decided to move West over to 61, the old blues highway and come in from that direction.

The interstate through the magnolia state had been empty, but the closer I got to Memphis, the more shells, abandoned cars, and small jams I saw. The road south from the city glittered like pieces of candy as sunshine bounced off windshields of stalled automobiles.

I assumed it would get worse, so took the rural two lane west.

I thought it was a good decision, and was congratulating myself as I turned north puttered up 61, and tried to decide if the 55 bridge or the I-40 Bridge was the best choice to cross the Mississippi.

Then I remembered the old railway trestle had been turned into a bike path that not only crossed the river, but ran through twenty miles of Arkansas and spilled out in a trailhead outside of West Memphis.

The eight-foot-wide trail would be all blacktop so the motorcycle could make it. There would be no cars to block the way through mostly wooded areas and progress would move unimpeded.

I twisted the throttle, jumped back up to fifty. Now that I had a plan it was just a matter of making it happen.

It took twenty minutes to navigate through town and see the two bridges lined up from the old steel museum on the bluff. From up there the pedestrian bridge looked clear while 55 was a parking lot.

I congratulated myself on a good decision as I raced down the hill toward the bridge.

I didn't hear the shot that took out the engine.

One minute it was whining, if not quite cranked into the red, a steady rumble roar that dulled the sense. The next minute it stalled, coughed and the pistons locked.

I fought a wobble as it slid to a stop, and that's when I heard him.

"Nice of you to finally show up."

The bastard was in a wheelchair made from a bobcat loader. One of the small one's used by landscapers in tight spaces, little more than a seat on treads with detachable blades that can be changed out.

He was strapped to the seat with a rifle in his lap and a line of his soldiers stepping out across the road to block the way.

How the hell had he found me?

"I bet you're wondering how I found you," he grinned and used the joystick to wheel forward.

His squad lock stepped behind him.

Son of a beach was psychic too. Did the fall give him new powers when I tipped him off a building in Alabama?

"You're building quite a reputation for yourself, Dad."

He grinned again.

I yanked the pistol, sent three shots his way and dropped the bike. One pinged off the cage around his bobcat but he didn't flinch.

I'd be impressed with the bastard if I didn't want to kill him so badly.

I lifted the rifle and sent a shot in his direction as fast as I could pull the trigger.

His men began returning fire.

Automatic weapons versus my seven shot Winchester.

It was no contest.

I started dodging toward some cover, somewhere back the way I came.

Except it was all uphill. Not even a decent bush to crouch behind. I bolted right and headed toward the river.

A baseball bat hit me in the back.

Or at least that's what it felt like.

I tumbled down the riverbank ass over elbows and slammed into the bridge footing. Bullets chewed into the concrete, dust and chips filling the air like snowflakes.

I crawled behind the concrete edge of the bridge as their bullets chewed away at my hiding place, and slithered out of the backpack. No hole all the way through. The cans, the padding had stopped the bullet, but left me with a bruise that was going to hurt for days.

If I lasted that long.

Their guns went silent after a moment, just the memory of their echoes and a cloud of gritty dust floating off in the wind.

"You want to give up," the General cackled. "Or us come in after you?"

They had the high ground. I remembered that lesson from one of the Star Wars movies. I've got the high ground Anakin.

I did not feel like pulling a Darth Vader, because frankly, I was already so close to the dark side Vader would be like, "Damn, that's an evil mofo."

So, I did as many men who had come before me had done and looked to the river for an escape. The brown muddy water was full of debris and muck from floods further north. It roiled and rolled against the black mud shore and shot downriver at twenty miles an hour or more. If I had a boat it'd be perfect. I could wallow off in the water and duck down as they tried to shoot the bobbing craft.

"My kingdom for a boat," I muttered.

There was the crack of a branch to the right of me and I aimed at the thick bushes and sent a shot into them.

It looked like the General got tired of waiting and was sending his boys to flank me. Which meant there would be another on my left, so I sent my last bullet that way and didn't let them hear me cuss when I ran dry.

I dropped the gun and ran for the water.

In the movies, it would have been a perfect dive, judges holding up ten cards as I knifed into the water and held my breath to swim far out of range into the middle of the river.

I'm not that graceful or lucky.

I took three steps into the muck before my boot got stuck and I tripped face first into the stinking mud. A bullet splatted next to me and I did my best belly crawl the last ten feet and spluttered into the water. Bullets churned up the ground and waves around me, and planted itself firmly in my ass, a million-dollar wound according to the Army. It burned in the nasty water. I dragged myself along the bottom as far as I could go and bobbed up to turn back to shore.

Seven soldiers lined the shoreline drawing beads on my bobbing head, and I could see them grinning. I didn't get a chance to see the General or the look of victory on his face as something plowed into the back of my skull and sent me under.

I came up sputtering next to a driftwood log, and grabbed on the backside of it, putting the log between the soldier's and my head.

Bullets chunked into the wet wood with a scratching plop and hit the water around me as I drifted out and away fast.

CHAPTER ONE

I could hear the General shrieking but couldn't make out his words as the log carried me along the river and Memphis rapidly shrank on the horizon.

CHAPTER TWO

I don't know how long I was in the water. I held onto the log until I couldn't feel my legs from the numbing cold, and when my hands began to slip off the water soaked log, I wrapped my arms around it tight and did my best imitation of a kick to reach the shore.

I should have gone for the Arkansas side, but the Mississippi side was closer and I wasn't sure I could make it all the way across.

There was a monument on the riverfront in Memphis to a man who rowed out in a shallow boat to save dozens of passengers from a sinking steamboat, and lost is life in the process.

I could have used his help as the cold sapped my strength and energy. I could feel sleep stealing up on me, and knew that if I closed my eyes, I'd drown.

But then my feet hit something and I began to stumble up onto a sandbar as the force of the water rushed me higher. Then

CHAPTER TWO

I was on my knees and crawling out until I was on a high portion of the mud outcropping.

I felt like laying down and sleeping then, but some primitive part of my brain must have still been working because I shoved up and crawled on hands and knees until I reached the brush at the shoreline. I kept moving up, forcing aside the kudzu planted there to prevent erosion, and crawling all the way to the top of the riverbank, twenty or thirty feet above the water.

Luck was with me then, because if the crumbling shore had given way and sent me back down, I don't know if I would have made it up again.

I rested at the top for a few moments that stretched into thirty minutes and must have napped because I jumped awake with a shock. I was too exposed out here, ready prey for any Z that wandered up.

I reached around and felt my backside to check on the bullet wound there. My numb fingers didn't go into any holes, but there was a long bloody gash that split the skin open. I'd need to pack it and give it some attention later, but I didn't have lead rattling around in my bottom, so that was a plus.

I moved into a squat and stood up, let the dizziness wash over me and threw up what felt like a gallon of river water, still brown and dirty. It left an oily taste in my mouth and that made me throw up again.

Just marking my territory.

But after the second round of vomiting, I felt a little better and stumbled through the woods away from the water.

The General and his men would be looking for me, and checking downriver, and if they had set a trap for me in Memphis, then he would assume I'd head for the next bridge in Greenville.

I had to figure out how he knew I was going to Arkansas

though, and how he knew to lay in wait on the 55 Junction.

I'd need food so I could think clearly, and a weapon to replace the one I lost. Weapon. Food. Shelter.

It was like a damn mantra in the post Z world. Food could come before weapon, but those were priorities.

I kept limping through the woods, using the trees for balance. My wet clothes were making me shiver and I added fire to the list of things I wanted. I wanted it before food, and before a weapon, but that was just the spoiled civilized part of me trying to complain.

Pain was inevitable.

Suffering optional.

I had run a couple of hundred-mile ultramarathon's each year before the Z apocalypse. They were an exercise in distraction, a meditation in pain management. One was in Chattanooga TN on a New Year's Day one year. The day started out clear and cold, and rapidly devolved into thunderstorms that soaked everyone to the skin, and turned three miles of the course into a slog through a flood swollen creek. The drop in temperatures made hypothermia a foregone conclusion for everyone, and hot soup at the aid stations a necessary survival tool.

But it was cold between aid stations. Wet cold that coated sore muscles and leeched into the bones so that you were left to wonder if there was ever such a thing as warmth, or if you would ever have that feeling again.

I felt like that now.

I couldn't feel my toes, or feet, just numb slabs of meat I kept propelling forward. My fingers were curled into fists, unable to move from the claw like pose locked in the joints. My hips ached, but at least they had feeling. Everything else just was numb, so numb even the shivering had stopped.

CHAPTER TWO

I kept moving forward, head almost down and knew I was going to be in trouble if I didn't find something soon.

And then I did.

A fishing trailer set back from a cleared acre to the shore. Empty. Boarded up, so it might be abandoned.

It was a single wide model from the 70's, covered in black grime from years of exposure, an empty wooden carport at one end of the porch. There was a boat under a second carport, a fourteen-foot metal long john with expired registration from a year ago.

So, it wasn't completely abandoned, just unused before the Zombies hit, and not since then.

I sent up another silent prayer and angled my stumble toward the front door. I almost didn't see the Z.

It came around the edge of the trailer and lurched straight at me, almost a mimic of my lurch toward it.

I moaned.

It moaned.

Then we collided and fell together, it's jaws snapping for my neck and face, my clawed hands shoving back against its chin, fingers just millimeters away from its slavering teeth.

Hands grabbed at the wet clothes and tried to dig through the swollen canvas material. I struggled to move, to get on top, to roll over and away, but my slow brain couldn't get my slower muscles to respond.

The Z pressed closer.

I shoved my clawed fist into its chin and pushed. I pushed until it's head bowed back from the taut rotten cords in its neck and I shoved even harder, until something cracked and it stopped chomping, stopped biting and I kept pushing until the head popped off and warm goo sprayed over my hands.

Then I rolled over, dry heaved and tried to wipe off the gore in the black leaves.

I realized I was crying, wondered when that started and forced myself up to the trailer. There was a padlock on the door, and I lifted one of the cinder blocks being used as a step and used it to smash the lock open. It wasn't easy, it wasn't pretty and I dropped it twice in the attempt.

But finally, the door swung open, and even through my river water stuffed nose I could smell the Z stink on my hands and sleeves. I couldn't take that in the room with me, and suffer through it all night.

I turned and shuffled back toward the river, remembered to double check my surroundings for more Z only after I reached the water, but it was safe for the moment. I splashed the cold water over my hands and sleeves, removing as much of the gunk as I could and hustled back to the trailer as fast as I could.

Daylight was fading and I wanted to check it out before it got too dark.

There were mattresses inside in the three bedrooms, and water in the tanks on each toilet. There were stale clean towels in a linen closet, along with old blankets that looked like they were just waiting for the owners to show up for a long weekend of fishing.

No weapons except for a filet knife and fishing gear with a firestarter, and the cabinets were bare of food. Until I reached the one above the fridge.

I didn't hold out much hope because people don't keep food in that cabinet, not always or often. It was usually stuffed with appliances or dishes that were only used on special occasions.

But this fisherman's trailer had an unopened box of saltine crackers, three cans of carrots, two cans of peas and two cans of cranberry sauce. It was a veritable thanksgiving feast.

I piled it all in the living room, then stepped outside. There was an overturned metal pan, like an old-fashioned wash bucket next to the boat. I'd check out the boat in the morning when the sunlight would give me the best view.

Right now, I just moved the bucket into the middle of the living room floor, gathered a lot of wood from around the trailer and stacked it inside and beside the bucket.

I shut the door, blocked it with the overturned kitchen table and stripped off my clothes. I built a small blazing fire in the bucket and when I was warm, hung the clothes across the shower bar that I moved next to the fire.

I sat naked in front of the flames, and cooked the carrots and peas into a soup, drank it all, ate a package of saltines with a can of cranberry sauce, and wrapped myself in a nest of towels and blankets to sleep, filet knife close at hand.

3

CHAPTER THREE

The next morning, I overslept.

I know that sounds weird in a world where clocks had no meaning. But ever since the Zombie Armageddon happened, I'd been pretty in sync with the rising and setting of the sun, waking up when it was first light, and ready for bed not too long after dark.

Not today.

I opened my eyes to full sunshine leaking through the windows facing east. It must have been a little after mid-morning and I cursed quietly because that meant the General would have had a head start on searching for me.

If they ran across this fishing cabin, I was toast.

I checked the clothes and they were mostly dry and smelled like smoke. I guess that's what happens when you burn a fire inside a washtub in a trailer and hang your pants over the flames.

It made me think Cowboys must have stunk pretty bad, and

then I realized most cowboys took a bath on Saturday unless they came across a river or stream, and even then, it was iffy. So, they must have smelled pretty much like homeless people all the time, except with manure and sweat and horse lather thrown in.

I took a second to appreciate the smell of only smoke and river water as I got dressed. I took the blankets from the nest and folded them in half, then slit a foot-long hole in the middle of that. I put my head through the hole and it made a blanket poncho. I did the same with two sheets tied them around my waist with a strip of towel like a belt. Now I had extra layers over my coat, and was prepared for any cold snaps that might happen if I was caught out without shelter.

Plus, I could fold my hands up inside the blanket as I walked and keep them warm. The temperatures were dropping into the forties at night, but never climbing out of the fifties during daylight.

The weather here was fickle. It could be seventy-one day and twenty the next and I wasn't enough of a weatherman to read the clouds.

Bundled up I slowly opened the door and stood back to one side, just in case anyone was lying in wait.

But no one was there. I stepped out into the world, slid the haft of the broken lock back into the clasp to keep the shelter intact in case someone needed it in the future, or if I came back this way with my kids, and went to investigate the boat.

A lot of fishermen store gear in their boats, but this was a weekend trailer in the woods and the boat was just a metal hull Sixteen feet, three unpadded seats, a rotten board on the gunwale where a motor could be mounted.

No motor.

No paddles.

Just the boat on a trailer with two flat tires and a path that led down the cleared lot to the edge of the river.

I put two packages of saltines and an open can of cranberry sauce in the bottom of the boat on a towel, double checked to make sure I wasn't missing any paddles hidden in the leaves or in the eaves of the carport. I tossed a line of rope into the bow, just in case, then lifted the trailer hitch and pulled.

It didn't budge.

I stood up and sighed, then moved the small wooden blocks away from both wheels and lifted again.

This time the boat scratched through the dirt and made a torturous run for the river. It was slow going, the flat tires grinding against the soft dirt of the path. I grunted and strained and had to stop four times as I dragged it downslope toward the water, but finally made it.

It took another five minutes to get the trailer turned around, and less than one to slip the boat off the back and into the water with a slapping splash.

I looked around to make sure I was alone, but all I could hear was the lapping of the water against the hull and birds in the trees.

I took that to be a good sign.

I shored the boat hull aground, searched for a board or branch, something I could steer with and came up empty.

I didn't have time for this. Who has a boat in a river shack and no way to steer it? No rudder, no paddles.

All I needed was a rudder really, a flat board I could hold in the water and steer across the current. The water would carry me downstream and over to the other side.

Not pretty.

Certainly, not efficient, but effective.

But I couldn't find a board outside.

I pulled the padlock again, went inside and started looking at the kitchen cabinets to take a door off the hinges.

Before I did that, I checked the bathroom and found a small shelf with a sixteen inch one by two board, which wouldn't work. Then I checked the back bedroom and there was a six-foot plank horizontal on one wall as a shelf.

I ripped it down. It was only a one by eight pine, lightweight and would do the trick. I checked outside again.

Still clear, so the shack got locked up and I got into the boat and used my new multipurpose rudder and paddle to shove off from shore. I sat on the back seat and played with the angle of the board in the water, twisting and shifting it to see how I could steer the boat and after a few moments had the hang of it.

I drifted out into the river, silent but for the water, watched the shore as it slipped away and shuddered.

A hundred yards from the shack a couple of dozen Zombies did their relentless march toward the clearing and the trailer. Some kids, mostly women.

If they had caught me out in the open with just the filet knife, I would have been in trouble.

Instead, I sent a silent prayer up to the river gods and anyone else who bothered to look out for me as I angled out into the water. The Z didn't even notice my passing.

CHAPTER FOUR

Mark Twain was a river pilot back before the Army Corp of Engineers decided to try and tame the mighty Mississippi. Still I couldn't help but think of him and old Huck Finn as I crossed the river in a flat bottom boat. Sure, Huck did it on a raft and Twain plied the muddy waters in a steamboat, but a sailor is a sailor no matter how far from shore, right.

I kept hunched over in the boat to minimize my profile for anyone who might be watching, conscious that the General and his men were still on the Mississippi side of the water.

Any crack shots in their unit could take me out fairly easily.

Twain called Helena the jewel of the Mississippi.

I'm from Arkansas and he must have been talking about the city during it's heyday, because what I knew about the Delta city did not suggest a jewel.

CHAPTER FOUR

I gauged I was ten miles north of that bluffs where the town looked down onto the water when I made landfall. There was a wetland creek that emptied into portion of the river behind an island. I began poling in the shallow water with the multipurpose paddle/rudder and now poling board and ventured up the creek until the cypress disappeared and the land turned to cotton and soybean farms. The creek became an irrigation ditch with shallow walls, but still wide enough for the boat and shallow enough to keep pushing.

It stopped at an earthen dike and I finally had to abandon ship. I used the rope to tie it off to a metal drainage pipe and flipped the boat over to keep out rainwater after dragging it out of the water. If it flooded, the rope would keep it in place, just in case I needed it again.

It was like the trailer I sheltered in the night before. I didn't want to destroy anything because of who might use it after me, or on the off chance that I came back in this direction and needed it. Boat, shelter, buildings.

There was a lot of destruction in this new world.

I was trying to limit mine to Z.

And the occasional militia man or bandit that tried to stand in my way.

I extra layers had worked well on the water, keeping me warm in the nippy breeze that blew steady from the North and west. I tightened the line snug and climbed out of the ditch to stand in the middle of a vast field of soybeans.

I checked the sun that was beginning to move toward the west and followed it so my shadow stayed behind me.

I walked for half an hour until I hit a tractor trail between the rows, a dirt path that sectioned off the overgrown farmland. It ran North, and I knew I-40 was in that direction so I didn't mind taking it.

Then I saw a centaur.

I admit I might have been tired, and it was a play of light across shadows and I don't know why I was thinking about a mythical creature from fantasy worlds, but I looked up at a bare road, glanced down and when I lifted my head again my first thought was it's a centaur.

In a world where zombies roam, then maybe more is possible.

Turns out it was a man on a horse. That made way more sense, at least until I saw Pan run out from the underbrush and if creatures of myth and legend were roaming the newly apocalyptic earth, I don't think they would make Arkansas their first home.

I wouldn't have.

I left the state at eighteen, but kept being drawn back in. First by the death of my mother, which brought me my first ex-wife. I dragged her to California and when she got pregnant, she absconded back to the natural state so our daughter could be raised near family. I followed and we had my son and a divorce.

A second dalliance gave me a second marriage and third child that created a move to Florida for job security with a growing company, and closer to her parents.

That divorce left me stranded in mid-level management at corporate America. I escaped in running, escaped in books, fell in love with the winter weather and planned to retire to a beach community after a run up the corporate ladder. I got to see my kids once a month in Arkansas, twice a month in Florida and I watched them be raised by other men.

My son became a hunter and fisherman, adopting good old boy habits learned from his step-father. My oldest longed to travel and I heard tales of her mother trying to squash that dream.

CHAPTER FOUR

And each trip back to Arkansas, I watched the changes as right wing conservatism drifted on a fine line with banana republic politics. It was number fifty out of fifty in almost every category measured. Education. Economic. Open mindedness.

Even the state's claim to fame as being natural was a marketing veneer as chicken farms dotted the landscape in the Northwest to supply the largest poultry company in the US, and hog farms destroyed the watershed of a dozen rivers.

The Delta region was abandoned as those who could afford it moved to Little Rock and points northwest.

That was good for me now, since I hadn't encountered a Z on this side of the river yet.

I thought going through Arkansas would be easy.

After all, I had just left Central Florida a couple of weeks ago whose population was higher than the entire state.

When I saw the man on the horse, I was a little surprised.

I stopped in the middle of the road and stared for a minute, wiping the cobweb memories of half man half horse from my vision and he started trotting toward me.

I waited, hand on the filet knife under the serape, which is the name of the way I was wearing the blankets I just remembered.

He pulled up on the reins about fifteen feet from me and rested his hand on a pistol grip holstered at his waist.

"Afternoon," he said.

Southern thick voice, face not weathered. Smooth skin like he spent more time inside than out. I couldn't see his hands but I bet they were soft. He was thin, but who wasn't these days, extra flesh hanging off his jowls and neck.

"Howdy," I said back.

A flash of anger at just how easy it was to slip back into the accent I'd grown up with, the one chipped away by years out in the world.

"You're trespassing," he informed me.

Hand still on the gun. Eyes flicking around behind me to see if I was alone, running point. No concern for what was behind him or around us.

"I'm just passing through."

"That you are," he said.

Still watching.

"Where'd you come from?"

"Other side of the river."

"You ain't got no guns?"

Part of a statement, partially a question. He noticed my hands under the blanket, noticed I hadn't pulled them out.

I did so then and held them up to show him they were empty.

"That's dangerous round here."

"It's dangerous everywhere," I told him. "But someone decided to take them up by Memphis and I went for a swim."

"You swim across the river?"

He didn't believe me.

"Found a flat bottom and floated."

He nodded.

"What you doing up in Memphis? There's a lot of the undead up there."

"There is," I agreed. "Looking for a way to cross."

"Yeah, they figure out how to use boats or swim and we're gonna be overrun over here."

He sat up in the saddle and stared across the fields. Maybe he could see something I couldn't from his higher vantage point.

"You ain't gonna make it off my land before sunset," he informed me.

"I can move faster."

"Nope," he said and wheeled his horse around. "Turn right at the next road you cross. It's gonna bring you to the house. I'll put you up for the night and then you get going in the morning."

"Thanks," I called after him as he began trotting back up the road. Tiny puffs of dust sent up by the hooves drifted back toward me on the cold wind.

The weather promised a change, something colder in the works, maybe even a freeze. I could see a line of clouds marching across the horizon like a solid wall of gray. I didn't want to be out in it.

But I wasn't sure I wanted to stay in a stranger's house.

He was a little too quick on the draw to offer shelter.

There was southern hospitality, and giving a room to a stranger was something my grandfather might have done. Different world back then.

Or maybe it was a different world now.

Maybe he wanted to know where I was on his property, and make sure he had me under control for the night and moved on in the morning.

I stood thinking about it for a moment, then decided I could consider the possibilities while moving just as well as I could playing statue. I started walking up the road, still damp hiking boots kicking up dust just like the horse.

I had decided to either keep going or turn left as soon as I found an intersection. There were too many scenarios that ended up with me in a pot, or worse going into his house. I'd just keep moving, watch out for being followed and get clear.

CHAPTER FIVE

There was a second man waiting for me at the crossroads.

I wondered if he was the devil waiting to trade my soul for a guitar lesson, but the deals old Splitfoot offered were always in Mississippi. He didn't travel much in Arkansas or Louisianan, but always in some dusty backwater on the east side of the Big Muddy.

That's how Highway 61 got its nickname. The Blues Highway ran along the birthplace of the blues, dilapidated cotton farms given over to sharecroppers too broke to be called poor. They scratched out a living from the soil, paid a landowner ninety percent of what they made for the right to do so, and turned to music for solace and relief.

Things so bad most of the time that they made deals with the devil just to escape. Sometimes just to eat.

I wondered what deal's Old Sam would offer now, and if this

was him.

"I'm Sam," he said.

I nearly pulled the knife, nearly sliced his throat and started running. It wasn't superstition, just one of those odd moments of coincidence that people attune to the Universe and God say is an answer to something.

Sam was a six-foot skinny man, dark skin with large white eyes. He wore simple work pants, work shirt and worn boots, leather gloves hanging out of one back pocket, a grimy bandana the other. He looked more like a farmer than the devil.

"Sam," I shook his hand.

He waited for me to introduce myself and when I didn't, started talking.

"Mr. Boles sent me down here to walk you in."

"Boles."

Sam nodded and started walking, just expecting me to follow. I glanced up the other two roads and briefly considered making a run for it.

But Sam could just go get Boles and tell him which road I took. A horse could catch me pretty fast.

So, I followed.

The man wasn't much older than me but moved with a slight limp, as if old age and suffering had taken control of his limbs. The average age of a person one hundred years ago, was forty something, and just before the Z plague wiped out the data scientists and bureaucrats who kept up with such things, the average age was seventy-two.

The average age now was who knew what, but the average time to live seemed to be short.

The group I was with lost half of our people in Florida just trying to escape. I kept them safe through Georgia and we picked up strays as we searched for a promised land to turn into a new home.

We lost more then.

There were just too many dangers in the new world and we were like pioneers struggling across the old paths, trying to make a place where we could live in peace, free from Z, free from tyrants and armies and criminals.

Sam was older than me and even I was past the age that was once considered old. I didn't feel old, not yet, but this new way of living was harder. It was tougher on the body. Almost starving, fighting, the adrenal glands working overtime to dump adrenaline in the body a couple of times a day, every time a zombie showed up, or a new person with a gun.

There were just too many ways to die now.

I caught myself and cursed silently. I blamed Arkansas. It had a way of making me feel morose, of turning me into a pessimist.

I knew better.

Back in the before, I spent a lot of time working on attitude. It may have sounded new age and hippy, but turns out how you talk to yourself and how you view yourself has a lot to do with the way our life is.

If you're a constant Debbie Downer, life is going to give you a bunch of lemons. It's what you expect and it's what you notice.

But if you focus on the positives, focus on the opportunities, focus on solutions, life gives you those as well. The more you focus, the more you find them.

Sam may have been tickling last centuries' definition of old age, but he was alive. He survived the worst thing to happen to the human population since the Black Death. He was moving. He had food last night, and food this morning and he was in Arkansas.

So did I.

So was I.

Little Rock was just a few hours' drive from here, even on country roads. I was in the same state as my kids, finally.

I survived so far. I was getting better at it.

Now I just had to find them, and I knew where to start looking.

Just needed to eat dinner, sleep with the knife under my pillow and take off at first light. I grinned. I had a plan and a goal. No devil could stop me now.

CHAPTER SIX

I shouldn't have been thinking about the Devil as we walked up to a farmhouse, but the oak in the front yard looked spooky, a simple tire swing creaking on worn rope twisting in the wind. It was an older home, but at least it wasn't wood and didn't look like something out of a horror movie.

If it did, I might have turned tail and ran, Sam and Scratch be damned.

But it looked like a simple brick ranch home, surrounded by a thick wooden fence like a barricade and I suppose that was what it was. The first line of defense against zombies.

Sam opened the latch and ushered me through the gate. I could see Boles sitting on the front porch in a leather wing chair that looked out of place.

He had his pistol in his lap, but his hand wasn't close to the grip. Not that it mattered too much. I was behind the fence and all I had was a thin filet knife for gutting fish.

Boles smiled and stood up from the chair.

"Glad you could make it," he took three steps down and met me to shake my hand, holstering his pistol as he did.

I pulled my empty hand out of the serape and shook back.

"I think Jean almost has supper ready, what you think Sam?"

"Yes sir," Sam didn't look at Boles.

"You going to go get the others?"

Sam nodded and shuffled around the side of the house.

"Others?"

Boles motioned me to follow him inside the house.

"We got about a dozen people here," he said and stepped through the door into a dark hallway.

The hair on the back of my neck was trying to send all sorts of signals to my gut, but the man had a gun. I gritted my teeth and stepped in after him. The ball of worry in my stomach unclenched a little inside. There was a light at the end of the dark hallway where it opened into a large room the stretched the length of the house.

I've heard of open floor plans, but this was one for an architect's digest. The ceilings were twenty feet tall leading up to a second floor. The back wall was all window looking out over a swimming pool, two pool houses on either side and a green pasture that stretched back to a row of trailers about one hundred meters away. The trailers were pressed end to end to form a metal fence and I could see people moving around them, in and out, smoke from fires curling up in a fog over the rooftops.

The back room had a huge stone fireplace on one end, and a kitchen on the other. A giant room that must have been twenty-five feet wide and twice that long.

Boles led me to a long plank table near the kitchen and offered me a chair with my back to the wall so I could see through the windows.

"Impressive?" he smiled and settled across from me.

I nodded.

"Nice set up."

"We've had to make do," he told me. "This wasn't my house. I just took it after... you know."

I did know.

There was a lot of taking after and not too many people around to object to the taking, especially in the Delta.

"We're safe here," said Boles. "As safe as can be expected, I suspect. Where you from?"

"I'm coming from Florida," I answered. "But I'm from Pine Bluff."

"Really?" he squinted one eye. "You don't sound like you're from here."

I worked hard to sound like I was from somewhere else, but I could feel the drawl wanting to come back.

"I've been travelling a lot."

"Why you coming back? Things are pretty bad out there."

"I'm checking on some of my relatives."

He nodded, like that was a wise thing to do.

"You heard much about Pine Bluff?"

I shook my head.

"They burned it down."

I wondered who he meant.

Pine Bluff had an arsenal for the disposal of chemical weapons, and a population that dropped from over sixty thousand when I lived there to just above thirty the last time I drove through.

Arkansas had a couple of militant groups, especially in the North part of the state. Did any of them come down and steal weapons? Did the Z overrun the city or did someone burn it down trying to fight the Z.

It was all passing curiosity, because while I might have to travel around Pine Bluff, my kids lived further north in Little Rock. I could stick to the more rural roads through England and up to Scott to find a way to cross the River. It was almost all farmland, much like what I walked through this morning.

Less people meant less trouble.

I just had to make it through dinner first.

A caramel skinned vision served us drinks. I watched the back of her in the kitchen as we sat, then she was behind me. When she brought me a glass of lemonade and set it beside me, I could smell violets and vanilla. I glanced up to smile.

"Thank you."

She didn't make eye contact, didn't nod or smile back. She placed a second glass in front of Boles. Same look with him.

Her shoulders were hunched and she moved like she wasn't trying to make noise. Wasn't trying to be noticed.

Boles reached out and ran a hand down the small of her back and across her round rump. Jean didn't flinch, but she looked like she almost lost that battle.

"Get our plates," Boles told her.

She hurried back into the kitchen.

I could see Sam through the window leading a group of people past the pool and down the sloping pasture toward the trailers. They were all black, dressed like him in simple work clothes, and shuffled like he did.

I heard the front door open and listened to two sets of boots clomp down the hall. Two giants stepped into the room.

I'm a student of history, or at least I was before the Z.

I read stories on a lot of different topics, articles and if I'm confessing, was a bit of a bibliophile. I would read an article about ancient people, how their average height was five feet, and dig into some other article about Vikings who due to increased protein from fish in their diet, could top six four, six five and literally stand head and shoulders over the villagers they raided.

Or world travellers, rare at the time who would wander from town to town in countries and carry with them stories of giant men they had glimpsed and seen. They never told tales about normal men, because after all, who wanted to hear a day in the life of a farmer? The villagers wanted tales of conquest, glory, battle and anything that pulled them out of their ordinary lives. Tales of giants would do that.

I thought all this because they weren't literal giants.

But the shorter one was six foot six inches and the one behind him was six eight or six nine. They were built like line backers, thick banded muscles, huge necks, bullet shaped heads and I could see they were brothers.

Dim eyes flicked to me and the first one stopped to stare. The second bumped into him and started cussing, a half word out of his mouth before he saw me and shut up too.

Tweedle Dumb and Dumber.

"Here my cousins," said Bole.

We locked eyes and I could see he wanted a reaction from me.

"What are you going to do when they hit their growth spurt?" I asked.

He grinned then and gave a quick guffaw.

Tweedle Dumb and Dumber glanced at Boles and started smiling like his laugh gave them permission. They moved to the table and set on long plank benches on either side, their bulk taking up a huge portion of the twelve-foot section.

"This here's Leon and Dion," Boles introduced them. "They been overseeing my workers."

Dion was the bigger boy and he pounded the table with a ham sized fist. Our glasses jumped, spilling lemonade.

Jean hurried over to the table with two gallon jars and set them in front of the big boys.

Tweedle Dumb, or Leon, but I think I was going to stick with my initial impression grabbed Jean around the waist and jerked her across his lap. He ran a hand up her leg under the plain skirt, thick white fingers on her skin like white spiders.

She didn't move, didn't flinch, just stayed where she was as he moved his hand between her thighs and rubbed. Hard.

"Act right Leon. We got a guest."

Tweedle Dumb turned two piggish beady eyes in my direction and grunted. He let go of Jean and pushed her off his lap, then smelled his fingers.

Tweedle Dumber laughed, and Boles shook his head in amusement.

"You know it ain't your turn tonight," he said.

Dumb grunted again.

"You just going to have to go down and get you something else," Boles continued.

Grunted again as Jean came back and slid a platter of beans, greens and cornbread in front of him. It was twice the size of a normal plate. She returned with a second platter for Dumber and placed a normal plate in front of Boles.

I got a bowl.

They tucked in with spoons, no preamble. Just slurping and scraping sounds as the three men shovelled food into their gullets.

I took a small bite.

Jean watched them while they ate, fear and loathing battling it out in her eyes. She was scared of these three men, and hated them.

After what I just saw, I couldn't say that I blamed her but it wasn't my problem.

We finished the meal, if not quite in silence then at least without talking.

"What do you think of them beans?"

"Hot," I told him.

Boles laughed. His cousins did not.

"I have Jean cook 'em with peppers we got from out back. You ready for the nickel tour?"

"I'd rather turn in if it's all the same to you."

He glared at me for a second, just a flash of anger, but Jean blocked the view as she cleaned the plates from the table. When she moved back, the smile was plastered on his face.

"He ain't asking," Dumb said.

Dumber grunted. I guess he agreed with them.

"Maybe a walk would help the digestion."

Boles pushed back from the table and led me to a set of sliders in the glass wall. He opened the door and invited me through first, then stepped in front of me once we were out. Tweedle Dumb and Dumber fell lockstep in behind me.

I tried not to feel small.

I tried to blame the roiling in my gut on the beans. But I can admit I'm not comfortable with a pair of giant strangers looming behind me. I kept a hand inside the serape on the handle of the knife.

I wasn't sure if it would do too much good against their thick blubbery skin, but maybe a couple of quick swipes across the forehead could blind them long enough for me to get away.

If they didn't crush me first.

I wanted a sling. And David.

And a tank.

Two tanks while I was wishing.

"We got about two hundred acres of soybeans out there," Boles pointed to the farmland that surrounded his ranch house. "When they come in next year, we're going to be sitting pretty on food and even have extra to trade."

"Smart."

"You darn right it's smart," he grinned. "I was an insurance salesman before all this. I even insured this farm. That's how I knew to come here once it happened."

"What happened to the owners?" I asked.

I didn't mean to say it. Not my business, I was moving on. But I got distracted staring at the line of eight trailers that formed the far end of the property and the people there, all women or almost.

Black women.

"They're over there," Dumb guffawed and pointed.

I followed the tip of his thick finger to a couple of fresh graves scratched into a patch of soil.

"Nice of you to bury them."

"It was the Christian thing to do," Boles smiled.

"Most people just leave Z where they fall."

"Z huh? That what you calling them?"

I nodded.

"Yeah, the Cartwright's weren't Z. They just thought they were better than me, that's all."

"Thought they was better than all of us," Dumber grunted.

"But I guess they learned their lesson."

Boles led us past the pool and toward the tiny collection of trailers. The women and four men stopped what they were doing and watched us approach. Sam sat by the fire and looked up from stirring the pot.

"Evening folks," Boles greeted them.

They stood in frozen silence. The women eyed Dumb and Dumber, the whites of their eyes showing, standing stock still as if they were frozen. Even the men didn't move. The two giants moved around me and waded into the group. They each picked one woman by the arm and led her back toward the house.

The rest watched them go.

The chosen bowed their heads, two of the men glared, but no one made a move to stop them.

"These fine folks help take care of the farm," Boles explained. "How's dinner tonight Sam?"

"Fine, sir," Sam didn't look up.

"Sam's in charge out here," Boles told me. "But he knows who's in charge of the whole outfit. Don't you Sam?"

"Yes sir."

"We all agreed to get through this together," the man put his hand on the handle of his pistol. "And we been doing fine so far."

I glanced up at the house as the two men led the women through the slider.

"It looks like it."

"Yeah we got ourselves a nice little set up here."

"I'll be moving on at first light," I told him.

Don't get involved. Not my circus.

He looked like he wanted to nod but didn't. I could see the three men watching me. Sam looked up from his pot of what smelled like stew.

CHAPTER SIX

If I could have made the fence, I would have run.

If I had a gun, I would have popped Boles first, then worked through the rest and sniped the giants as they ran through the door.

But all I had was a thin nine-inch blade with a dull point.

"A nice little set up," Boles said again.

It was one of those situations where everything felt off, surreal. Sam was watching me, Boles too. I could feel all the eyes of the crowd on me, the air thick with tension or anticipation.

I tensed up and tried to plan it out. How it would happen, who would make the first move.

Maybe I watched too many westerns growing up, the gun-slingers facing off in the dusty streets in front of the saloon, violin music ratcheting up the tension, camera tight on the eyes as they squinted at each other and waited for the first one to draw.

Then they didn't.

In the movies, they did. Noon o'clock high was the time to slap leather and take out some hombres. But on the farm in Arkansas, Boles just laughed.

The tension was gone, evaporated like smoke from the fire.

He began walking toward the house and I fell in beside him, our steps crunching in the worn grass and dirt.

"I can put you up in the guest bedroom," he said. "Long as you don't mind a little noise from the boys. They can get a mite rowdy."

"I won't be bothered," I told him. Noise or not, I wasn't planning on sleeping much tonight. If I could have managed the one eye open trick, I would have done that. Or I could just sneak off at three in the morning, get outside the fence and make it off his land before sunrise.

They were selling too much crazy here. The vibe was off, like I'd stepped back in time. Was he running a slave farm?

I almost asked. More information might clear some things up. Maybe it was something in the smoke, or food or just being back in the state. The Delta had always been rich in history, which was a department of tourism's way of saying old norms and ways were still in effect.

Better for me to move on than worry about what was going on here.

Boles pointed to the last door of three in a short hallway.

"That's your bunk."

"Thank you."

He waved and disappeared to the other side of the house.

I walked past the two doors that bracketed the hallway and heard grunts and tiny cries of pain. Like they were competing with each other.

I could stop it. I had the knife, I had the advantage of first movement. A quick bust through the door, a couple of swipes and then set up an ambush when his brother came to investigate.

They would have guns I could use on Boles when he ran across the living room. I could take their weapons and his horse and make the two hundred miles to Little Rock.

I didn't.

I moved past the door to the third.

Jean was turning down the sheets. She jumped when I stepped in.

"You scared me," she said.

I had that effect on a lot of people since the Z apocalypse. Scarred head, dead eyes, and just my face. A monster's face when I looked in the mirror.

I closed the door behind me and watched her sigh. She thought

I was going to bend her over or push her back on the bed, I guess. Take a quick ride.

There was no fight in her eyes, just resignation. As if she expected that was what she was there to do.

"What's going on here?"

She looked up at me.

"What do you mean?"

"You have them outnumbered. Why don't you fight back?"

"They have guns."

The sigh again.

"I could show you how. Tell you how," I corrected.

"You could do it."

I shook my head.

"Not my problem," I told her. "I'm moving on in the morning."

She folded the edge of the sheet with a crisp corner.

"That's what I suspected. Come in here and spread ideas, and then just leave. The communists used to do that."

She had to be a decade younger than me, maybe half that over again.

"What do you know about communists?"

"Russians," she lifted her chin. "And Koreans. Spread their ideas about a perfect society but they didn't have one, and they couldn't make one."

"I'm not talking about what's perfect," I put my back against the wall so I could watch the door and the window at the same time. Jean moved in the periphery of my vision.

"I'm talking about what's right."

"What do you know about what's right and what's wrong?" she finished the bed and paused at the door.

She was right. I was a stranger passing through and somebody trying to keep me from my goal, some unseen dark force maybe, kept putting these things in my way. These things that had nothing to do with me.

Things that were keeping me from saving my kids. Or finding out the truth.

"Nothing," I told her and it was everything. She heard it in my voice.

"Don't come out here at night," she warned. "No matter what you hear. No matter what you think you want to do. It's better if you stay inside."

She opened the door and I could hear moaning, and cries of pain. The sound of fist hitting flesh from the two rooms that bracketed the hallway. My palm itched on the handle of the filet knife.

Then she shut out the sound with the click of the doorknob.

I could still hear them in my imagination though. I slept with my boots on.

7

CHAPTER SEVEN

I heard their bootsteps in the hallway around two am but didn't have time to do much before they were through the door and on me. Tweedle Dumb and Dumber each grabbed a leg and pulled me out of bed. I landed hard on the floor and banged my head against the nightstand.

They dragged me down the hallway, through the living room and outside into the yard. Boles was waiting by the pool and sent a couple of well-placed kicks into my ribs as we passed him.

The knife was gone, lost in the bedroom. The serape was bunched up around my neck, choking me as the two giants hauled me across the rough concrete surface and onto the cold grass.

Dumb dropped by boot and fell on my chest with his knees sending the last of my air out in a whoosh. Dumber grabbed my arms and cinched them tight in a rope. He threw it over a low hanging oak tree branch and the two men hauled me up until my boots couldn't touch the ground.

I was swinging like a piñata, and then the two of them took turns whacking at me with ham sized fists to see what candy they could get to fall out.

They were disappointed.

Boles stepped in after what seemed like an hour and ripped the serape and shirt off my body.

"Seems you been talking out of turn," he glared at me.

I could see over the top of his head. The harems from the trailers had gathered to watch, Sam standing over them on a box. Watching them. Watching me.

"We have a good thing going here," Boles yanked the rest of my shirt off and delivered a solid right to the gut.

It hurt.

"And you're trying to mess it up."

Kidney punch. It spun me around, cinched up the rope on my wrists and cut off circulation.

If they would just give me a minute, I could try to think of something. But my ribs hurt. My kidney hurt. My skin hurt.

Boles stopped my spinning. I faced the tree, couldn't feel my hands.

"Lord all mighty, what happened to your back," he let out a low whistle.

It was still striped pink with healing scars from the burns, new tender skin prickling under the cold breeze.

He reached out a long fingernail and scrapped it across one of the wounds.

I'm not ashamed to admit I screamed.

Howled. Not much difference. It hurt.

Then he kicked me in the small of the back. Or one of the

giants punched. Or they brought a mule out and let it do the job for them.

It started the spin again, and I could see the crowd, see Sam as I swung back and forth, round and round.

Dumb punched me to reverse the spin, Dumber hit me to reverse it back.

I caught Sam's eye during a rotation, watched a sliver flash snick across his throat and lost sight of him as I whirled around. He was gone when I flicked back.

Somebody laughed.

I think it was Boles.

Then it turned into a gurgle and he was on the ground, throat leaking blood under my boots as I twisted and turned over him. Dumb hopped one way, Dumber the other, and the women in the crowd surged toward them.

It wasn't much as fights go.

The two giants punched and fought, but the women howled like banshees and threw themselves on the them. The three men left joined in. Dumb and Dumber took a few hits then turned and ran off into the darkness. The crowd surged after and I was left spinning from the tree branch in a slow lazy circle.

Boles under me. Sam over by the box.

And then Jean in front of me, my filet knife in her hand.

She stopped the spinning and reached up, but couldn't touch the rope. She set the knife on the ground, went for the box and dragged it over. That let her reach the rope and she scraped the thin blade against the thick rope until it parted and dropped me in the dirt under the tree.

I tried to work the knots free, but my hands wouldn't cooperate.

"Let me," she bent in front of me and sawed the strands apart.

"This was all your idea."

I shook my hands to get some feeling back and struggled to get up. She stood back and watched. I guess that's all the help I was going to get.

Boles was leaking under the tree, his legs still moving as the nerves slowly died and his body shut down. I bent down and rolled him over, unbuckled his pistol and strapped it to my waist.

The lynch mob drifted back toward the oak tree in silence.

"They got away," one of the men told Jean.

He glanced at Sam's body lying in the dirt, let his eyes drift over to Boles then up to me. They rested on the gun for just a moment.

"You're in charge now," I told her in front of them.

"Not me," she pointed to the group. "They can take care of themselves."

I looked at them then, a ragged group of survivors and started walking back to the house.

"You can have the house tomorrow," I told them. "I'm leaving at dawn. Until then stay out."

I almost shut the door on Jean, but she pushed in past me as I pulled it closed and locked it. She followed me to the front door where I checked the bolt, and shifted a giant buffet in front of it. It might not stop a giant from kicking their way through, but it would be noisy and slow them down.

"Guns?"

It was my turn to follow her as she led me into the giant master bedroom. There were a couple of gun cabinets against the wall that looked like new additions.

"You slept in here with him?" I asked.

"Some nights," she shrugged.

"And you never thought to get a gun and shoot him in his

sleep."

"People get used to things when they feel safe," she said as if it was the way of the world.

I suppose it was. Like cooking a frog in a pot of boiling water. Turn up the heat gradually and the frog won't jump out, just cook as it gets used to the heat.

It's the same in any relationship, I thought as I grabbed two rifles and fitted them out with ammunition. I wanted to take them all because I wasn't sure what I would run into heading into Little Rock, but I also didn't want to leave the survivors unprotected. Two of the eight were a good compromise, plus a buck knife, and two boxes of bullets.

"I'm going to come with you," said Jean.

"Nope."

I don't think she expected it.

"What do you mean nope?" she squeaked.

"Nope. It means no. As in N O."

"No? But I rescued you."

"You rescued all of them. You rescued yourself."

"And you."

How do you argue with that? Ten minutes ago, I was strung up in a tree playing the role of punching bag like an Oscar contender.

"Yes," I said. "Thank you."

"So, I'm going."

I thought about saying no again, but decided to save my energy. I'd just get up before her and leave. No argument. I just nodded my head as I started digging through the closet looking for clothes that fit.

"What happened to your back?"

I saw her staring at the scars in the mirror.

"Grenade."

"Somebody blew you up?"

"Tried to."

"That what happened to your head?"

I reached up and touched the scar tissue in my hairline.

"Somebody tried to shoot me."

"You pissing that many people off?"

"It happens," I shrugged. "Your guy was ready to shoot me for walking across his cropland."

"He wasn't my guy," she spat. Ice in her voice.

"Bad choice of words."

"The worst," she said. "When I told him what you said, he was royally pissed off."

Ouch. The bruises on my ribs were courtesy of her. Surprised I didn't put that together sooner.

I slid into a thermal undershirt and layered a thick flannel on top. They almost fit.

"Did you know he was going to hang me up?"

"He's done it before. Sam talked him into getting rid of one of the other men so the three left could have one more wife."

"That what they call them?"

"They call them what they want. Harem. Wife. Sister wife. They got the idea off the television from Mormons. Said we were going to repopulate the earth. But mostly the men didn't want nothing to do with the women after the boys were through with them."

I pawed through a section of closet with winter clothes looking for a jacket.

"I heard."

"They were rough," she shuddered. I guessed even the memory of it was bad, then recalled the way one of them pawed her at dinner.

"Can you pack us food?"

Might as well get her busy before I snuck out.

"I'm not going out there alone."

I let my hand drift to the pistol grip.

"Is there another way in the house?"

She shook her head.

"We could hear them come through the door, or break a window. But who knows what kind of guns they have out there. I know they kept a deer stand stocked for hunting and killing."

"They can see the house?"

"The back of it."

I almost ran out to tell the others to hide, but Jean stopped me.

"They'll be inside," as if reading my mind. "They know about it too. If they decide to just start shooting, we'll have to hide."

I decided to wait out the morning in the bedroom and shifted the dresser over in front of the door. The window couldn't be helped, but I sat on the floor with my back to a wall so I had a clear view.

Jean propped up beside me.

"You want to have a go?" she asked.

"Go where?"

"A ride? A poke? Sex."

"Now?"

"You're giving me a ride out of here, I figured I'd return the favor."

Was that the world we were in now? First Anna, now Jean. Who else was trading their body for favors and safety? Was that the world my daughter was a part of now? Both of them?

"No."

"I didn't get with Boles if that's what you're worried about," she said.

"I'm not worried."

She scooted closer to me, her hot leg against mine as we watched the window.

"I've never killed a man before," she told me.

"I've killed plenty. It doesn't get easier. I'd avoid it if you could."

She nodded, but I could tell she wasn't listening. Her eyes had a faraway glaze to them. She lipped her lips with the tip of her tongue.

"You may not want a ride, but I do," she said, her voice husky.

She reached over and began to unzip my pants.

I thought about fighting back, I thought about arguing.

But she bent her head into my lap and I gave in without saying a word.

CHAPTER EIGHT

She woke up before I did in the half light of dawn creeping through the windows. I knew she was awake because her fingers were doing things inside my pants again. I let her.

When it was over and done, the sun had peeked over the tree tops and we lay in a satisfied puddle.

"We need food," I told her. "And a gun for you."

I wasn't planning a long future with her, but damn if the woman hadn't earned a ride.

We dressed, and I helped her layer up.

"The extra clothes can keep them from biting you," I explained.

"I've been behind these walls since the beginning," she told me. "Not much call to interact with them."

"You know what they are?"

"I've been to Haiti," she grinned. The corners of her eyes

crinkled when she smiled. It looked like she hadn't done that in a long time.

"Haitian zombies?"

"Voo Doo has a long history of bringing back the dead," she explained. "There are more believers down in New Orleans. Or were."

I let her reflect on that a moment. I don't know what happened to the Big Easy or any large city in the US. All the small towns I had been through, and Orlando where I started were bastions of the undead now.

Or survivor compounds.

Were was probably the right choice of word. No matter what they believed in before.

"I studied up on it," she told me as I shoved aside the dresser and we checked the hallway. All clear.

The sun lit up the backyard and the two dead bodies still down by the tree. No one was stirring in the trailers yet. Still too early.

Good.

We could pack up and get going before they woke up.

Jean led us into the kitchen and we packed up two bags of food, enough for several days.

"Does he have a car?"

"Truck," she said and pointed to keys hanging on the key rack.

I nudged open the garage door and checked. A pickup truck was on the other side of a Buick sedan, both covered in dust.

"When's the last time they were started?"

She shrugged.

"Boles used the horses because they don't need gas."

I grabbed the keys and checked the truck. It fired right up despite the dust and the fuel gauge was full. I loaded in the rifles and groceries.

"I'm going to open the garage door," I told her. "Drive the truck out."

She shook her head.

"What if they're waiting to shoot me?"

I hadn't considered that. I thought that since the deer stands were in the back, that's where they would be. But I realized that waiting to ambush the front would be smart too.

Except it was Tweedle Dumb and Dumber.

I didn't know if they would consider it. They seemed to have a one-track mind during our interaction at dinner.

"I'll drive it," I moved to get into the cab. She pushed me back.

"I'm not afraid," she said. "I just want to know the possibilities."

She dropped the truck in gear and stood on the brake while I opened the door. It reached the halfway point and she ducked down behind the dash, eased her foot off the pedal and coasted forward until she was clear of the garage.

I checked outside, but we were clear, so I shuttled the garage door down and jogged to the driver's side.

"Budge over," I told Jean.

"I'll drive."

"Not yet."

She glared at me and huffed, and I knew she just wanted to prove herself to me.

"When we get off the land," I told her. "Stay down."

Maybe she saw wisdom in that, or maybe she was just happy to be free, to be escaping and going.

She slid across the seat and kept below the dashboard. I dropped the truck in gear and followed the driveway out to the crossroads.

I wondered if Sam met Old Scratch last night, if he and Boles were keeping the devil company now as I turned to the north. A Z wandered across the soybean field and stopped to watch us pass. It didn't give chase and if it moaned, the sound was lost in the wind through the open window as we kept driving.

9

CHAPTER NINE

No one shot us as we left. No one shot us as we travelled down the dusty road through the fields.

After a few miles, it felt dumb to keep ducking so I sat up in the seat. Jean took a cue from me and sat up as well. She curled one leg under the other on the seat and leaned against the door.

"Which way you going?"

"We're north of the river now," I explained. "I think through Stuttgart and shift north to move down from Lonoke."

"My people are downtown."

"I'm hunting in the suburbs. Sherwood."

"You can drop me closer than that."

"You can have the truck."

That seemed to satisfy her and she settled back into the seat and let her head droop against the window.

The sun came up behind us, spreading golden rays across the

road in the direction we were headed. I was surprised there weren't more cars.

I guessed people here hid in their homes while the world went to hell around them. Growing up my grandparents were self-sufficient, a result of their Depression era upbringing. I can't remember a time they didn't have a garden, or fish in the freezer, or deer meat.

They shopped at the store, especially for Sunday dinners to grab potatoes and other veggies they didn't grow on their own. But we always had green beans and pinto beans and homemade jellies my grandmother canned by hand.

Tomatoes for stews, soups and spaghetti so good I haven't tasted the like since. Muscadine for jams and wine, blackberries. Pecans from eight trees around the yard.

I remembered many Saturday nights sitting on the sofa next to my grandmother as we watched television and shelled pecans, crushing the shell with sliver nutcrackers and picking out the meat with tiny silver picks that looked like dental tools.

She was fastidious, her eyes glued to the set while her hands worked with practiced ease. My child like fingers were different, less sure.

It hit me as I was driving that she always gave me a separate bowl, and it was because of the shell fragments I would get in the pecans.

She would go back after I was done and clean up the mess I made.

That made me smile.

Maybe there would be more survivors here, people like my grandparents who were better prepared to ride out any sort of plague. Zombies would be problematic, but not something any good old boy couldn't handle with a couple of rounds from a hunting rifle.

We passed through tiny bergs and small townships, collections of houses and more trailers than tornado alley deserved.

But no people.

No zombies either.

"Where did they all go?" I asked aloud.

"The people?"

"The people. The zombies. We're almost to Stuttgart and we have only seen one Z."

"Z? That what you call them?"

"What did you call them?"

"Zombies. Haitian Voo Doo Zombies."

"Are you Haitian?"

"I'm as American as you are," she said. "But that's where zombies come from. Everybody knows that."

"I didn't know that," I told her. "I thought zombies came from someone's imagination, and made a movie. Then some government superbug got loose and started all of this."

"Maybe," she said. "But you said you were from Florida, right? I went there once. That's the only place I've ever seen a superbug. A cockroach in the hotel room. You walk in and that sucker starts flying."

"Palmetto's," the thought made me grin.

The first time you encounter one is terrifying. She was right, you walk up to squash it with your shoe and it takes to the air.

Every time it happened, my kids would run around the house screaming, full of the willies and laughing at how spooked it made them. I'll confess that I may have ducked and run from several in my time too. I draw the line at shrieking though. Manly yells for help, maybe, but shrieking? Not me.

"Cockroaches," said Jean. "That's what I called them growing up and no scientific name is going to make them any different. It's like these damn zombies you want to call a Z. Like giving it a pet name. That's not for me."

Pet names. Z. Palmetto's. Plague.

I'd called it a lot of things in my head, and in some conversations with Brian and Anna. Apocalypse. Armageddon. End of the world. But Jean had me wondering about labels.

And wondering who made it, who caused it all to happen.

Who unleased the second of the four horsemen?

Or was it the third?

10

CHAPTER TEN

It's easy enough to think Arkansas is all backroads and back woods and sometimes it does feel like that. Just as quick as you can think there's nothing there but farmland or pine forests, the woods open and a small town straddles the road.

I had been through a hundred of these on the journey here, maybe more. The towns were little more than a collection of houses, sometimes a post office, sometimes a store.

I road in the cab of the truck, pistol in my lap, rifle across the seat and passed through, Jean snoozing with her head against the window.

Some of the stores were intact, shuttered and locked. I thought about stopping and cleaning them out, filling the back of the truck bed with supplies.

Just as quickly I discarded that thought.

A moving truck was a juicy target for anyone who wanted a prize, but they might let it pass. A truck full of supplies was too much temptation.

Better to keep it empty, mark the township in my head and plan to find more when I approached the city.

I was worried about bridges.

In Florida, the bridges were jammed as people tried to escape. I hadn't seen that in smaller streams and rivers, at least until I reached Memphis and the bridges across the Mississippi. But here they were empty.

I chalked it up to population. Arkansas was just not that crowded, the people congregating in the Central and Northwest part of the state. From the Delta, up through Little Rock there just weren't that many people.

On the one hand, it was good.

The Z were scattered and spread. I didn't have to worry as much about the Zombie infestation as we did before.

The bad part was it made finding supplies and survivors even harder.

I had a small debate when I ran across Highway 79. I knew that ran through Pine Bluff, the small town where I grew up.

Burned, Boles had told me.

But where did he get his information? I really needed to stop being so bull-headed and just ask the people I met what they knew about other parts of the world.

I didn't turn though. I kept going North until the road ended and turned left to head West.

Eventually I'd hit Interstate 40, and would parallel it through Lonoke, then work my way north and west again to approach the suburb of Sherwood from the North. The kids had their home in the suburbs. Maybe I'd luck out and they would be hiding in their house.

Two months.

CHAPTER TEN

That's how long it had been.

And I'd been busy. Hiding. Running. Saving other people.

What if something happened to them while I did that?

What if I couldn't find them. What if they were just gone?

I tried to swallow the lump in my throat, but it stuck there. I couldn't breathe and had to stop when my vision swam in tears.

I gripped the wheel so hard I thought it would break in my hands, or my knuckles would snap.

"Give me a Z right now," I bit back a sob and let my head fall against my forearms.

I gave in for just a moment, let it wash over me, the grief, the anger and frustration. The ball of rage I kept in my stomach threatened to overwhelm me, not with anger but with hatred.

I hated myself.

Hated the divorce, the million lost moments. The not being there.

It was a cascading list of failures that dropped like dominos, a bunch of what if's and should have's. I let them come, let them drown me, until the noise of it all dropped me down and spun me around. The feelings receded and left me empty, hollow.

But alive.

And in Arkansas. An hour from the kids, maybe two.

An hour from answers.

If I just stopped feeling sorry for myself in the middle of a country road in a pickup truck I stole from a dead man.

The laugh didn't even sound real coming from my throat. More like a chuckle. A weak chuckle.

I killed the owner of the truck when he tried to kill me.

I had killed a couple of dozen men, maybe more, when they tried to kill me. When they tried to stop me. Hundreds of Zombies.

I glanced into the mirror at my red rimmed eyes, scars on my cheek and head, face drawn like a skull.

I couldn't second guess everything that led me to this point.

The Z plague wasn't my fault.

All I could do was lift my foot off the brake and get moving.

So, I did.

I'd find answers somehow.

And if I had to rip apart the entire state to find them, it wouldn't be that big of a loss.

11

CHAPTER ELEVEN

Driving through the delta region is an exercise in time travelling. There are some towns that seem untouched by progress. The roads roll through the farmland, dotted with occasional expanses of pine forest and a small twenty-four-inch green sign announces the town or city limits as you roll through.

One stop light, one store that may or may not have a grill attached, a couple of trailers perched on the banks of the blacktop, or wooden clapboard houses that survived fifty years of tornados only to be destroyed by families moving on for better opportunities in the big city.

At one point before the zombie Armageddon changed the world, I was going to work on an executive redevelopment committee to bring work, life and vitality back to the region.

I had applied for the position in hopes of being closer to my children here, and it allowed the freedom and flexibility to travel back to Florida to see my younger daughter. There would have been things I'd miss about the beach life in the sunshine state, namely the beaches and sunshine. The natural state of Arkansas could be considered an outsider's paradise with hiking trails, bike paths and plenty of space to run, float, camp and play outdoors.

It didn't have beaches though, unless sandbars on the river counted.

The search committee decided to go with another application, and I didn't get the chance to rebuild or rehabilitate the state.

Which is sad.

I think a visionary could really take control of the Banana republic of politics that is the government and do something, like set an agenda and mission to move from number fifty in everything all the way up to forty-five.

It wasn't the way things worked out though. I was thinking those thoughts when the tire blew out.

We heard a loud hiss and then the truck began thumping and pulling hard to the left, trying to carry us across the road and into the woods.

I didn't bother to pull over because who was going to come along the highway. I just stopped and we got out.

"Got a flat," Jean told me.

"I noticed."

She squatted on her haunches and stared at the spare bolted to the undercarriage of the truck.

"Spare's flat too."

I glanced around check our surroundings. Did someone shoot out the tire? Were we in a trap that hadn't closed yet?

Jean ran her fingers along the flat tire to show me the tread.

"It was thin to begin with," her strong fingers plucked a nail from the rubber and held the sharp point up for my inspection.

"Then you ran over this."

Like I did it on purpose.

There were two things I always hated about Arkansas roads. Nails and rocks. That same corrupt government was in the pocket of the trucking industry through their generous lobbyist groups, so dump trucks and construction crews littered the road with rocks, debris, nails and screws.

It created a sub industry in the state of windshield repairs, which created their own lobby group to work with the trucking industry so they could stay in business.

It meant most windshields had chips and cracks, and everybody had a flat at least once a year. Sometimes more.

I always wondered if they could have used the money to buy tarps and cleanup crews instead of paying legislators, but politicians were the same in Florida and California where I had lived pre-Z.

Look in the dictionary under corruption and the word politician is printed next to it. If it's not, it should be.

"Guess we're walking," I told her. "We're not too far from Stuttgart."

The last mileage update was from a hotel billboard sign that told us it was only five miles ahead, so I knew it would take about an hour if we didn't find another vehicle along the way.

Jean grabbed our food pack, we holstered up and began marching along the side of the road.

I wondered for a moment why it wasn't the middle, but didn't say anything. She seemed lost in her own thoughts as well, perhaps thinking about what she might find in Little Rock.

I wondered the same myself.

CHAPTER TWELVE

The road made a slow shallow S curve as we meandered at a steady pace toward Stuttgart. In the winter, the fields were flooded to create wetlands and ducks migrated to the region every year, making it one of the duck hunting capitals in the United States.

Stuttgart built the city's reputation on that label, and kept the wetlands growing each year. They held a festival in honor of the ducks, built up large sporting goods stores to support the hunters, and created a nice little strip downtown to hang out after limits had been reached.

When visitors came in on the main highway, it led straight to the downtown area. We weren't approaching from that direction.

We heard them before we saw them.

The low moan of Z carried on the wind through the trees. It

sounded like a distant freight train at first, and I wondered if trains were still running. If so, who was driving them.

I slowed my walk, and noticed Jean slow beside me. Eyes up, head on a swivel we moved up the road and rounded the last curve.

The asphalt stretched out in front of us through the rice paddy fields that surrounded Stuttgart and made it a duck hunter's paradise. Every fall farmers would open the irrigation gates and flood the fields to create shallow ponds perfect for migrating ducks.

This year, I guess they got the gates open just in time for the Z to show up.

The two-lane road that cut through the middle of what looked like a mile of rice paddy was raised from the land around it. That was a good thing because we found the source of the moaning.

A hundred Z were trapped on either side of the road, up to their knees in mud and muck. Their arms waved, and reached, but they were stuck, unable to move from the shin and in some cases the knee down.

They filled the edge of the field just off either side of the road like a gauntlet.

Jean moved to the center and I didn't let her stay there alone for long.

"I guess this is where all the Z went."

She shivered. I didn't blame her. I wanted to shiver too. I wanted to shimmy and shake the willies off and run down the center line screaming.

Instead I just kept walking forward.

"We're going through that?"

I didn't turn around.

"I'm going through it," I told her. "Stuttgart is ahead, and we can find a car there."

"We can go around," she said.

I kept walking.

"Or we could just keep walking," I heard her jog up behind me.

"Going around would take too much time," I explained.

I almost couldn't talk though. We were moving at a fast clip. Just because I had to go through a tunnel of the undead didn't mean I wanted it to last a long time. At least they weren't walking.

The sounds of their moans grew louder as we passed and they swayed and pressed toward us. They almost looked like reeds.

One Z near the road leaned forward so far, his legs snapped and he plopped face first into the mud and grass on the edge of the field. Then he began crawling after us.

I was pretty sure I could outrun him.

But it set a bad example, because a couple of other Z were shoved forward by the herd, and the noise of snapping legs followed us like branches cracking in a thunderstorm.

And once they fell, the Z dragged their bodies after us on elbows and hands, clawing up the side and onto the road.

"I can't even," Jean gasped. "Crawling Z."

"Night of the crawling Z," I huffed out next to her.

"It's daytime."

Got to love the pragmatics in life, even if it's a post zombie one.

It was easy to outpace the crawlers but we paid too much attention to them and not enough to where we were going.

That's my only excuse.

We were focused on the crawlers as we ran past a sign that told us we were in the city limits, ducked up a side street and

CHAPTER TWELVE

right into a street fight.

CHAPTER THIRTEEN

I've been ambushed. I've been bushwhacked. I've been hijacked. That's all since the Z showed up, and none of the times it happened involved the walking dead. It's always been people, what's left of people that are causing problems.

I remember reading once that judge a person by how they act in a crisis if you want to know their true nature.

Since the apocalypse, I haven't really liked people's true nature.

I especially haven't wanted to look in the mirror or spend too much time thinking about mine.

The things I had done would make the old me shudder.

It might even make the old me stand on a soapbox and talk about justice and incarceration and death penalties.

Once I found my three children, maybe went back to Fort Jasper or maybe to some island in the Keys, I would sit down with a six pack and think about it.

Of course, by then I might have more to think about.

A lot more.

Like the scene we stumbled into.

Four people surrounded by eight guys. Never good odds. A silver haired older man, a woman and two teen girls. All dressed head to toe in layers. Unarmed. Scared.

The eight men were rednecks. The worst kind. Dirty. Scruffy. Cackling with mad laughter as they surrounded the small group.

They had guns, rifles and shotguns that they jabbed the man and woman with, and leered at the young girls.

I grabbed Jean by the elbow and pushed her back toward the corner we had just rounded, but it was too late.

One of the rednecks saw the movement out of the corner of his eye and spun around. He sent a shot in our direction, and it zinged off the brick of the building, showered us in debris and dust.

I dropped to one knee and aimed.

Three shots got three of them. The others bolted without shooting back. I got two more as they ran away, and the silver haired man grabbed a fallen rifle to join in. He shot two more.

The last one was smarter than the rest and disappeared down a road.

"Damn," Jean whispered beside me.

I turned the rifle on the silver haired man. We had just rescued him, but adrenaline was pumping and tempers were high. He might determine we were a threat and decide he didn't want to take any chances.

He swung the rifle around on us, then lowered the barrel just as quick.

The woman of the group clung to the two girls, all three of

them sobbing quietly.

"You friendly?" the man asked.

"Friendly enough."

I got off my knee but kept my finger on the trigger.

"We're sure glad you came along. Thank you."

"You were lucky we were passing through," said Jean. "They didn't look like they had anything good planned."

The man nodded toward the two girls.

"One of them went to school with my daughters. That one," he pointed to one of the first ones I shot. Half his head was missing, but the girls didn't seem that broken up about the loss of their classmate.

One left the clutch of her mom and started gathering the fallen guns.

"Do you have a car?"

I watched his hand tighten on the rifle butt.

"They tried to take it," he said. "Used nails in a board across the road to blow out the tires."

Damn, I thought.

I was going to ask for a ride. Or take their car, but now that they said the rednecks ruined it, we'd have to make an alternative.

"Let's go see what we can find."

I started walking further up the street, but didn't bother to see if they followed.

14

CHAPTER FOURTEEN

The town was empty. Or a better explanation was it had been cleaned out. There were no cars in any of the parking lots that bordered the highway that cut north through town. The used car lots were empty, the windows in most buildings busted out, trash and garbage spread across the roads.

The rednecks had been busy.

I bet they had a huge stash of stuff hidden somewhere. I didn't have time to go search for it.

The silver haired man's name was Roger. His wife was Barb, and the two girls were their own. A complete nuclear family in the after-Z world.

Rare.

"Where are you going?"

I asked as I led them through town. I kept my head on a swivel, studying, watching, in case the rednecks had friends. In case I could see something out of the ordinary, like a car. Hopefully one in a parking lot with the keys still in it and a full tank of gas.

Jean trailed after me.

She didn't grumble, didn't complain, just kept pace. I could feel her behind me though, a quiet storm of bottled emotion. Either we weren't moving fast enough or she didn't like the addition to our party.

I wasn't too happy with the speed either.

We needed wheels fast.

"There's a rumor about a place in Louisiana," said Roger. "Supposed to be safe."

I didn't think that was true, but what did I know. America was a big country, and the government had to have safe zones. Communication was down, but when they got it back up again, they could direct survivors to walled compounds while trained people cleaned up the mess.

Although I was trained by practice, I'm not sure if I would help if they asked.

The government probably caused this. Why would I clean it up for them? Once they were back in power, or once I turned power back over to them, they would just put a tax on what I did so they could live safely. Or safer.

I shook my head to rid the thought.

I'm not an anti-government nut, but I couldn't see an advantage to our former republic that rewarded the rich, punished the poor and worked hard to keep the classes stratified.

It's always been like that, since people started gathering in cities. It's been called the haves and the have not's, the nobility and the serfs, the birth of the middle class so they could feel superior to the serfs.

There was a myth of the self-made man that pervaded our

culture before the fall. A thousand new millionaires were created by real estate, then hedge fund managers made billions by sending them all into the poor house. A couple of thousand more people were made paper rich with a tech boom, then the super-rich colluded to make the market crash after walking away with billions of their own.

It made me wonder about the new societies I had encountered. Soldiers ruling by might. Kid's ruling so adults couldn't ruin it. The power of the sword replaced by the power of the gun, the power of the pike.

Yes, I was sure the rich were still out there, still alive and hiding behind walls. Using guys like me to clean up their mess.

"That would be nice," I told Roger.

No need to be rude. No need to bust his bubble. Let him pursue his dream of a safe place.

"There," he pointed.

It was an old service station with a three-bay garage attached to the side. The windows were covered in dust, but the angle of the sun glinted off glass in one of the bays.

We jogged over to the station. The inside had been gutted, empty food racks thrown on the floor, the glass coolers busted open.

The great thing about open windows was there were no Z inside.

We couldn't tell with the garage. A door led to the auto bays from the store, but it was closed. The glass was smeared with something, chocolate, blood or feces, or maybe just dirt. It was hard to tell which.

I tried to lift the garage door.

Locked from the inside.

I banged on it to see if we could draw any Z toward the front.

Nothing showed.

"Guess I'm going in."

I lifted the rifle and got it ready. Jean moved to one side so she could get an angle on the door. Roger and his brood spread out. If anything ran through the front door, they would have time to move.

Smart.

I guessed Roger and company hadn't survived that long by being stupid.

The door knob was crusty, but not sticky. I winced as I turned it and pulled the door open.

The smell inside was dead body, rotting meat, gas and oil. It smelled like Z, or roadkill.

I banged on the inside door too and stood back to wait.

Nothing came.

The light through the front windows was weak, casting a pale glow through the room. I could see the dark shadow of a car up on hydraulics, and another truck further past. If there were two vehicles inside, we were lucky. If they both ran, it would save us a fight.

I ducked my head into the room and out again quick, in case something snapped at me.

Then I stepped inside and shuffled through to the garage. A small bar was the only thing locking it to the tracks. I twisted the lock and threw open the garage.

I guess I was used to the smell.

When it washed out over Roger's daughters, they both turned green and emptied their stomachs. There wasn't much too it. They hadn't eaten in a while, but the dry heaving was going to leave them sore.

Roger stepped up next to me and pointed.

CHAPTER FOURTEEN

The dead smell wasn't from a Z. It was a body, a bearded man with a rotund belly and a Pollack painting on the wall behind his head, courtesy of a shotgun at his feet.

Jean slid in and picked up the weapon. She opened the breech to check the chamber and snapped it closed with a snarl.

The garage owner must have used the last one to take his trip to the other side.

Roger moved to the car on the rack.

"Think we can get it down?" I asked.

He nodded and went to the wall.

"No electricity," he explained, "But there's a release."

I watched him reach around behind a machine and move his arm. The car started lowering to the ground with a loud hiss of air. It landed on its tires as the hoist clattered to the concrete floor.

"Worked at a gas station when I was in high school," he explained.

He went over the car, popping the hood and checking the engine.

"Look for keys on a rack."

Jean slid in behind the driver's door and cranked the engine. It turned over with a few clicks but didn't catch.

Roger rooted around on the back wall and found a battery charger, but no electricity to charge it.

He went to the truck and I almost stopped him. But then he was under the hood and pulling the battery from it. He attached it to the cables in the car.

"Try now," he called to Jean.

She cranked the key. The engine thought about quitting. The battery was low, it clicked four, then five times. Finally, the engine caught with a cough, and roared to life.

Roger closed the hood.

"Pull it out."

She did and stopped in front of the garage. Roger walked around checking the tires, but it looked solid.

He motioned Barb and his girls into the car.

"You want to ride with us?"

"I'm going north," I told him.

He was watching my hand, his finger on his gun too. Maybe he expected me to try and take the car.

"You can go with them."

"I told you my people are in Little Rock," Jean answered.

"There's nothing north," he told me. "Someone told me Little Rock is all gone."

I nodded.

"I'll check on it."

"We're going to the safe town in Louisiana. We could use your help."

Finger still on the gun, but asking for help. Afraid I might take his car, grateful for my help earlier. I could see he was torn.

"We may come look for you after we go there," said Jean. "Zombies."

He followed her long finger as it pointed up the street. All the Z weren't trapped in the fields. Three were lumbering up the road, drawn by the banging and the car engine. One of his daughter's squealed.

"Get them fed," I told him. "Get them safe."

"You have to come with us now."

I turned and ran back to the truck. Old garages like this had to have more batteries. Tires lined a rack on the back wall, different makes and sizes.

Jean jogged in with me.

CHAPTER FOURTEEN

"He said he won't wait."

Even as she told me I could hear the squeal of tires as he raced away from the garage. The movement might draw the Z after him. Still, I hurried.

"Look for a battery."

She checked the shelves, shoving stuff aside and hooted in triumph.

"Found one."

I hefted it into the truck, connected the cables and sent a prayer to the Universe as she slid behind the wheel.

"No key."

Damn it.

"Check the visor."

She folded it down, but no luck, and began digging in the console, fingers searching the floorboard.

I ran to the wall and searched for a keyboard, a pegboard, anything that the dead man might have put the key on. It was blank. I went inside to the cash register, checked under the counter and shelves.

Nothing.

I kicked the shelf with my boot and broke it. Business receipts, trays of screws and the detritus that collects under registers spilled onto the floor, adding to the mess.

There was a key on a floating keychain in the middle of it.

I grabbed it, ran it out to the truck and passed it to Jean.

She shoved it in the ignition, cranked it. The engine caught and turned. The truck must have been in for a new muffler because it sputtered and screamed like it didn't have one.

"That's going to help us sneak across the country," Jean smiled.

I didn't care. We could blow the horn the whole way, crank

the radio as loud as it would go.

All that mattered was we had wheels, we were just over an hour away and we could go.

I jumped in beside her, finally letting her drive and used my back seat driving skills to direct her out of town. She weaved through the Z as they filled the street and set our course for Sherwood.

CHAPTER FIFTEEN

"You're pretty good at killing," Jean said. "I knew some men, boys really, back before the zombies that were in a gang. They had killed before, but they didn't take to it like you did."

Like I did.

It took a zombie apocalypse to discover my special talent, and it was something that would put me behind bars for life in a different world.

I remembered reading about killers in that world, men who took to a life of crime, or authors trying to share something they learned from cops. Most people only killed one person, and it was someone they knew in a crime of passion.

The ones who could murder more than a single person were rare, despite what news would have you think. Those who could kill as many as I had were rarer still, falling into a category called serial in the civilian world.

Soldiers were different.

They were trained to think different, and unless they were snipers, couldn't normally keep track of their kill ratio.

Which made me wonder what I was?

I wasn't a soldier.

I wasn't a serial killer, or at least I didn't kill for fun.

I just did what had to be done.

And it came too easy, too fast for me to know what was happening, and when I realized it, I tried not to think about it.

If you dwell on the numbers, it gets worse.

Like thinking about the past, and reliving all those moments where something should have been different. I called them ghosts.

Ghosts were real, and they haunted you, but it wasn't a spook in a sheet with two eyeholes cut out.

They were memories, as real as the feelings they caused. Sometimes hard to banish in the dark, fed by firelight and boogiemen fueled under the stars, or hidden in the shadows.

"I just do it," I confessed. "I don't think about it."

Because thinking about it would drive me crazy.

"It's probably best you don't," Jean advised. "Maybe it's something you have a natural talent for doing."

"Maybe."

"Or you hate people."

Maybe that too, but I didn't say it aloud. I didn't think I hated people though. I had done too much to save some along the way. I guess what I hated were bullies. People who used their strength, their power over others.

Kept them as slaves.

Kept them as objects.

CHAPTER FIFTEEN

Bullies like my stepdad. That's what started it, started the rage. Growing up poor, wearing second hand clothes, reeking of cigarette smoke that covered the house in a miasma. Kids at school were cruel. Always.

One pair of jeans to wear every day, new for the school year, and a second pair at Christmas if we were lucky. Growth spurts were the worst. They created highwaters, hems that drifted higher over the ankles. No pants to replace them though, because they still fit in the waist.

And if the waist got tight, half servings for supper so we shrank.

Imagine being punished for growing. Starving until you fit in clothes that were too small, too short.

The kids at school bullying because you brought half a sandwich for lunch, wearing pants too short, because you smelled.

I bottled it up. I bit my quivering lip and sucked it up buttercup, because that's what you do.

The jeans became shorts for the summer.

That's what you do, make good of a bad situation.

And now, if the situation turned bad, sometimes it took killing the bullies to make it better.

That's why I didn't play with the ghosts. I could have been a psychopath. The expression was, there but for the grace of God go I.

I'd heard about childhood friends who had gone to prison, who had turned to crime, had done their one murder and been behind bars.

I was too stubborn to go down that road. I bottled it up and hid it, and played by all the rules.

That fed the rage too, every time I saw someone breaking the rules. I had to follow them because I feared the consequences.

Why shouldn't they?

"I don't hate everyone," I told her. "You're alright."

She smiled. White teeth flashing in the sun coming through the window of the antique car as we puttered along the backroad toward Sherwood.

I liked it. The wind. The smile. The miles almost gone, almost home.

That's the best ghost to find, and worth fighting for. Moments. This moment.

We were ten miles from home and I found myself happy.

Take the moments when they happen. Store them up to fight the night.

CHAPTER SIXTEEN

Sherwood was empty. Front doors stood open in every other house, debris and things scattered in the front yards. A few were burned to foundation, stone fireplaces all that remained. The fire department was gone, levelled, as were the apartments built around the golf course.

We had to drop the car at a traffic jam on 167 where the road crossed under the highway. Too many people trying to get away, too many autos clogging the arteries, the shoulders blocked, the median blocked.

It looked like Florida.

"Careful," I whispered as we coasted to a standstill and got out. We both held rifles at the ready. I unbuttoned the holster on my hip.

Zombies liked to hide in wreckage.

"We should have made pikes."

"What's a pike?"

"A guy I was with invented them," I told her. "Long poles with blades on the end. Quiet killing."

She nodded like she understood.

"They don't like noise."

She did understand.

"We're going to move fast," I told her. "Try to keep distance between you and the cars. Watch where you step."

We had a little food in the backpacks, and we should have scavenged as we went. But I ignored my own rules as we rushed in a speed walk past the pile up, past the blocked roadway, the hospital that looked like a war zone. Windows smashed in the fast food restaurants. The sporting goods store.

We stayed on the service road, moving at a quick clip and I pulled up short.

"What?" she lifted her rifle and stared around, searching for danger.

"The RV dealership," I pointed. "It's untouched."

She shrugged.

"So?"

I shook my head. An idea for another time, but it was a good one. If we could find an RV and outfit it, we would always have shelter, always have a place to sleep.

Not now though, and not this place. There was no way we could pull one of the campers onto the road.

The bridge over the swamp was blocked.

"We have to crawl over."

She nodded and took a step on the grill of the first car, used it to climb onto the hood. She glanced around and ducked fast.

I stared, trying to see what she had seen, but her perspective was four feet higher than mine.

CHAPTER SIXTEEN

"I don't think they saw me."

The moaning grew in volume, suggested otherwise.

"They're coming," she snarled.

"Go!"

I jumped up after her and we hoofed it across the hoods and roofs of cars, across the cab of a truck, through the bed and down beside the roadway again. A dozen Z were on this side of the bridge and angling in our direction.

They were trapped on 167, but hit the guardrail, flipped forward and slid down the slick grass to crash into the side of stalled cars. Then they were up again, moving toward us.

We jogged faster, dodging between cars, over them.

I thought for a moment to break some gas tanks, try to set a wall of fire between us like I tried on 1792 in Florida.

That hadn't turned out as I planned. Brian and I created a mile-long string of cars that detonated in rocking explosions that shook the earth.

It was an accident. I swear.

Jean screamed as a zombie hand skittered from under a car and swiped at her feet.

I smashed its head with the rifle as it peered out and we kept moving.

We were making too much noise, jogging fast now, but the zombie moaning drew more zombies out of hiding. They were coming toward us now, blocking the narrow paths on the roadway.

"There!" I pointed her to a parking lot. It was a church, the lot was full, which meant two things.

Either parishioners were trapped behind the glass doors, their eternal slumber turned into a walking dead nightmare, or the people got tired of waiting on the road and decided to wait in the lot. Or park and make a walk for it.

We ran behind the building and through a vacant lot. The side road wasn't as gridlocked, letting us move faster.

We ran toward my old neighborhood and saw the damage. Fire station gone. Apartments gone. Houses burned.

I wanted to sprint to their home.

But didn't.

I couldn't breathe. I couldn't think, and I needed to think, needed to be calm because even though we gained some ground, Z were on our tails.

So, we walked.

Fast.

To the end of the cul de sac.

I stopped in front of their house. My kid's home with my ex and her husband. Their stepdad had been in their life for ten years, maybe more. Put them to bed every night in that house. Read them stories. Ate dinner, watched movies, taught my son how to hunt, how to fish. Taught my daughter about being there.

All the things I couldn't.

All the things I didn't.

The front door was shut.

"That it?"

I nodded. I couldn't speak.

The moans behind us got louder again. Zombies didn't quit.

We had to go in. There were two options. The house was empty. Or it had zombies in it. My zombie kids.

I swallowed. Hard. There was a lump in my throat. I wanted to throw up. I wanted to cry.

I balled it up, tamped it down.

Time for that later.

Right now, we needed to move.

CHAPTER SIXTEEN

The front door was locked. They kept a key under a potted plant on the table. I had seen my children use it a hundred times dropping it off.

It was still there. The lock turned. I hid the key again, just in case.

Opened the door. Knocked.

It was dark inside. No light through the thick curtains.

"Get in," Jean whispered, glaring at the zombies moving up the road now.

I knocked louder.

"No one's home," she said and pushed.

She couldn't move me. Nothing could. Not yet. I had to know. Were they inside, were they Z?

"It's empty," she shoved again. "Can't you feel?"

She was right. Empty houses have a feeling to them, I had known that. I could have felt it sooner if I wasn't occupied with other thoughts.

I stepped in, she followed and slid the door shut. She locked us in total darkness.

I had never been in the house before, but knew the layout from the kid's description, and from watching the exterior every time I drove up.

There were windows in both rooms that faced the front of the house. I moved right, smashed into a wall.

Felt my way into the room and crashed into a table. Worked my way to the curtains and pulled them aside.

Jumped.

A zombie stood at the window staring inside. It pressed against the glass as I moved back into the shadow beside the window.

The pale light leaked into the room. Jean followed and didn't bump into anything.

"Can they get through?" her voice was a whisper.

It felt right to speak in hushed tones.

"Not yet," I lied. They could. We had just bought a little time. Time enough to explore.

She followed me into the great room, a kitchen living room combo that stretched along the back of the house. I pulled the curtains away from the slider and flooded the room with light from the outside.

It was empty, but had been used. Maybe recently. The trash was full of cans. Water in a bunch of containers.

And a note scribbled on the wall.

It read, DAD.

I started crying.

17

CHAPTER SEVENTEEN

She let me cry. I fell to my knees, cradled the rifle and watched the message blur as tears dripped onto the carpet.

"Dad, we are alive and living at the school where we went as kids. Come find us there. Love you."

Written in my daughter's handwriting, painted with a sharpie. Like she was drawing a mural on the wall.

They were alive.

Jean let me finish. It didn't take long. I didn't have time to blubber. There were kids to be found.

I wiped my face with the back of my hand and stood up.

"Do you know what school they're talking about?"

"Catholic school downtown," I said as I checked the cabinets. They were empty.

"They must have run out of food, and went looking for a safe place to stay. I met some other kids who hid at a school too."

Byron and his group of children who turned his high school into a fortress.

"Let's go," I jumped up.

"Wait," said Jean.

Wait hell. I'd been waiting on this for weeks. They were alive, or at least had been when this note was written. It had to be fresh because the trash didn't stink.

Thinking of stink made me go back to the slider and check the zombie in the yard. Was it my ex?

Did my kids trap their mother in the back yard?

It didn't look like her, as far as zombies look like the people we once knew. Sunken features, gray skin, gray hair, black teeth. But the hair was long, and the shape different.

The Z moaned and bumped up against the glass as I looked past it to the broken fence. Just a neighbor then who wondered in and got stuck.

"You know her?"

Jean asked from my shoulder.

I tried not to flinch, tried not to jump and failed. She giggled. It sounded cute on her, and out of place.

"Neighbor I guess," I shrugged.

"How far to the school?" she asked.

"Ten miles. Maybe eleven."

She peered up at the afternoon sky, gray clouds covering everything with a dingy glow.

"We might make it before dark," she offered. "But we'd need to find shelter if something's wrong or doesn't go our way."

She was thinking it out. Which was a good plan. If I ran down the road unprepared, it could lead to disaster. In a normal world, I'd hop over to JFK or the Interstate and make an almost straight shot into Downtown North Little Rock. Their school was close to the river, and the drive would take fifteen or twenty minutes tops.

But the interstate was blocked as we had seen.

And I didn't want to explore a major urban corridor in twilight. Too much potential for danger, for damage. I didn't travel half way across the country to screw it all up at the end.

I wanted to punch the glass and shove a shard through the Z's head.

Instead I reached up and pulled the curtain closed, then stepped back.

"Good choice," she said and rubbed my arm.

Then she gave me a hug because I guess I looked like I needed it. She kissed me on the cheek, and then since our lips were so close together we kissed a little more. It lasted for a few minutes and she stepped back, eyes glistening.

"Looks like they ate all of the food," she nodded to the cans in the trash.

I nudged my backpack.

"We can make do."

I let her set up a couple of cans and went searching the garage for something we could build a fire in, a piece of metal or trash can, or even a bucket.

"Come look at this," I shouted.

She pressed up against my back to peer over my shoulder.

"That's going to make tomorrow a lot easier."

The kid's step dad had a lot of toys, boats, campers for hunting and even a Gator the Boy bragged about learning to drive on. Those were all at a deer camp in the woods east of here, and I sent up a silent prayer that the kids didn't go hide there because I had no idea where it was.

Sitting in the middle of the garage was a four-wheeler ATV.

I checked the gas gauge, which had a quarter tank, and searched under the shelves for a red plastic container. I didn't find more fuel, but it was enough to get us downtown so I didn't worry.

I did find a fire pit stuck in the corner in an unopened box, and dragged it inside.

Jean watched me open the box and set up the pit in the middle of the floor in front of the sofa. She looked at me like, congratulations now what can you burn?

"I know, I know," I grinned and began searching for wood.

I broke apart a shelf, a dresser and a bookcase and we were set. I didn't even feel guilty about destroying their stuff, since the bookshelf had once belonged to me a long time ago.

We ate canned beans warmed in the flames and Jean pulled a couple of books off the floor from the newly demolished shelf that we perused by firelight. I thought about the legend of Abe Lincoln learning to read and write by the hearth, and wondered about cowboys, and history and what people did before electricity.

Jean had an instinct for the answer.

She reached over and fumbled with my gun belt, but I helped this time. I set the belt within reach and slid my pants down to my ankle. She shimmied out of hers and climbed on top of me, one hand working magic as she squeezed and pulled. My hands worked too, one running over the solid curves of her muscled legs, the other stroking and teasing.

Then she pushed me inside her as she straddled my hips and rocked back and forth. I saw her look around the room and it made me think some more. I never would have pictured doing this in the living room where my ex raised our children with another man.

CHAPTER SEVENTEEN

It distracted me and I was glad it did because what we were doing felt good.

She must have thought so too because a few moments later, she clenched up and so did I. Then she fell forward to rest against my shoulder.

After a minute, I felt something warm drip onto my cheeks.

"You're a nice man," she snuffled. "Why couldn't I have met a nice man like you when this all got started."

She didn't want an answer and I didn't have one to give. We sat there in the quiet house our juices mixed and trickling out to spread across me, and listened to the crackle of the flames. Her breathing went slow and regular as I shrank and slipped out, and closed my eyes to fall asleep with her.

CHAPTER EIGHTEEN

When I woke up, Jean was gone.

I didn't hear her leave. I scooted toward the garage door in the kitchen and checked, but the ATV was still there. My hearing isn't as great as it was before all of this started, after all people kept shooting guns near my ears, tossing grenades at me, and there was an unfortunate incident with a highway full of exploding cars, but that totally wasn't my fault.

Still I'm sure I would have heard an ATV roar off in the middle of the night.

I stumbled back into the house and noticed my backpack was gone. And my rifle. And my gun belt.

Before this all happened, I was very good at keeping track of my things. But since the Z showed up, people just kept taking my stuff. It was starting to make me pissed.

Hunting rifles and weapons were easier to come by in

CHAPTER EIGHTEEN

Arkansas, but that didn't mean I wanted to waste all my time searching.

I pulled open the slider curtain and looked past the Z bouncing off the glass to check the fence.

Wood.

Wood would not do, not for what I wanted.

I tried to recall if I could remember a chain link fence on JFK, at least eight feet high. If I ran across one and it was safe, I'd stop to take a pole. I would have to find a machete later, and the wire to wrap the end and turn it into a pike.

I could go house to house in the neighborhood, but decided to get moving instead.

The truth of it was, I wanted to get to the kid's school. I'd burn down Little Rock hunting for new weapons with them by my side, but the thought of them only being five miles away left me lightheaded, and scared.

They expected me though. That's what I told myself.

The note didn't say Mom. It didn't say their step-Dad's name. It said Dad. Me.

I slid into my jacket.

It was all I had left.

I went into the garage, but there were no windows in the door, just a solid sheet of metal. I didn't want to lift the garage and find a horde of Z waiting to snack on me, so I went back to the front room in the house and peeked through the window.

All clear.

I went back to the garage, started the ATV and cranked it up. Then I lifted the door, rolled out, and dropped it back down again. No use in leaving the house open to weather and wandering Z.

We might need it again, or some other traveler.

I wondered about Jean.

She hoofed it out of here, but would I run into her on JFK? She said her people were in Southwest Little Rock and there were only so many ways to cross the Arkansas River.

Six of them, but four of the bridges were within blocks of each other downtown.

I kicked through first and second gear as I made my way across the side roads toward JFK.

If I saw her trying to cross, or ran into her, I might say something. But she did leave. That was her choice, and her reason.

Maybe it wasn't my place to wonder why.

Besides, I'd been planning to leave her over in the Delta. I almost left her in Stuttgart.

She was gone, my kids were close.

I shrugged it off and decided to concentrate. On the road, on reaching the kids, on watching for roaming Z. Jean could take care of herself, or she couldn't. Her choice to make.

CHAPTER NINETEEN

JFK meandered south from Sherwood into North Little Rock. My first wife and I lived in Park Hill off the main corridor when we bought our first house, and I drove past the small brick bungalow on Ridge Road since JFK was blocked in a lot of places.

It was a meandering route that carried me to and from the route as I tried to go around stalled traffic, crashes and spots that were impassable because of iron and steel walls made of wrecks.

At the top of Park Hill I stopped to stare at the Little Rock skyline. The kid's school was five miles away, closer to the river where it cut through town. The ridge I was on was known as a hill, but it really was the first of a series of ridges that led to the foothills of what eventually become the Ozarks.

Little Rock itself was nestled between two ridges, one to the South of town, and this one on the North side.

JFK stretched into the downtown corridor of North Little Rock, past a National Guard depot and the what once was the new high school. They were both gutted now, cars smashed bumper to bumper between them to create a sea of scorched hoods and shattered glass.

There was no way the ATV was getting through it.

I wasn't sure I could even walk past it.

I backtracked to Ridge road and took a side street down into the Levy neighborhood and found the River Trail spur.

Arkansas like a lot of the country took old railway tracks and turned them into bike paths. This must have been one of the spurs that ran north into Jacksonville, deeded to the city and parks and rec installed an eight-foot wide black asphalt path.

The trailhead to the road was blocked with two iron posts, but that was no problem for the ATV. It fit easily between them, and I had a clear path that ran behind the ridge straight under the Interstate and into a line of cars on Percy Macon drive.

The rail trail here merged with the road, signs directing cyclists and joggers back to the main road, but I could maneuver around the stalled cars using the sidewalks and parking lots that lined the streets.

I reached four cars tipped over on their sides and wheeled the ATV to the curb. The front left tire popped up on the concrete and a sledge hammer smashed into the engine block, flipped the four-wheeler on top of me.

I don't know if you've ever had a two-hundred-pound kick to the giblets, but it does not feel good. Stars popped behind my eyes, wind whooshed out of my lungs and other places I didn't even know I could breathe and a dull deep ache throbbed between my legs.

I heard the echo of the shot at the same time I glanced at the engine housing. Something big had blown a hole in the side of the steel.

Fifty cal was my first thought and that made me ignore the pulsating wave of pain radiating from my groin and crawl.

I crawled for the wrecks, trying to get my brain to work on directions. It did, too slowly. Lucky for me, another bullet gouged a trench in the sidewalk in front of my face, showering me with chips of sharp rock and dirt.

It let me know the shooter was on the right, and yep, he had a big gun. A very big gun.

Why he was shooting at me I would try to figure out after I put something between the two of us. Preferably something solid, and three feet thick.

I settled for a ditch.

It wasn't a ditch so much as a depression in the grass between the sidewalk and a building where years of rain runoff had lowered the level of the ground as it raced toward the street.

I barely fit, and hoped my wounded butt did not hover above the ground, too tempting for the shooter.

Ground erupted by my head and splattered black soil across my bloody face.

Nope.

He was going for headshots, and the dirt wasn't enough to stop the bullet.

I did my best impression of an Olympic sprinter and shot out of the blocks, dodging left and right as I made for the building.

He wasn't a trained sniper, that's for sure.

He didn't lead me, or anticipate where I was going. He shot where I was, and missed by half a second. Maybe less.

I heard the buzz of bullets.

I felt the tiny sonic boom whiz past my head.

The zing of thuds in the dirt behind me, around me in short bursts until I put the brick wall of the building between us.

Then two shots into the brick that crumbled the edge of the wall.

After that it was silent.

I tried to picture what I had seen in that direction as I passed the road. A hotel, four stories high would have been the best vantage point. Unless he was at the stadium for the high school, shooting from the bleachers. A good scope could give him that range.

Was he moving now? Adjusting his position to catch me when I ran from the side of the building, crossed the road to the next?

I decided to change the rules.

The old rail trail ran parallel to working tracks, empty of a train now. They led to the railyard in downtown North Little Rock, and from there crossed a trestle over the Arkansas River into Little Rock.

They also ran four blocks from the kid's school, albeit through what was once a really bad neighborhood.

But could the gangs be worse than the zombies?

At least I'm sporting colors, I snickered as I wiped blood from my cheek. Red. I didn't know if that was Crip or Bloods, but it had to be Bloods, right? Blood is red.

Then I couldn't remember whose territory the neighborhood was in, and that was okay.

I ended the self-debate with a sprint toward the tracks, down a ditch and a mad clawing scramble up the side. I pitched over the rails, and ducked behind the other side, putting a nine-foot mound of dirt between me and the shooter.

It must have caught him by surprise.

He sent a shot my way, but it was over the top of the mound, which was over my head.

I glanced up the tracks and saw I could stay behind the hill and stay safe if I ran hunched over.

So, I did.

For a hundred yards until I reached a road crossing.

Then I heard the footsteps.

I turned just in time for Tweedle Dumb to plow into me from the other side of the tracks, a huge mass of muscled flesh that lifted me off the ground and slammed me into the ground.

I thought the ATV punch to the jewels hurt.

This was worse.

He sent a kick into my hip that punted me five feet. I kept rolling, trying to use the hill and momentum to put distance between us.

"Found you," he growled and rushed me again.

I wish I could say something elegant about the fight. Something from the Matrix or a Saturday afternoon Kung Fu flick where I leaped into the air with the grace of a ballerina, spun around as if on a string and delivered a toe point that stopped him in his tracks.

But a real fight is ugly.

And sometimes accidental.

I got halfway up and lunged out of the way. Physics took over for him. I couldn't think of the formula, Mass x Speed equals he tried to veer after me, but I was too lean, he was too large. Something happened and he tripped across my ankle.

I felt a twinge, like a sprain.

He fell forward and couldn't get his hands up fast enough.

Sometimes when road crews in Arkansas were planting signs, they would use concrete to hold the steel bar in place. Later crews would come behind them, and when they couldn't dig the concrete up, just used a saw to cut the steel off a few inches above ground. It was lazy, yes, and time plus the elements would dull the end of the steel post until it was little more than a nub, a bump only a lawn mower could go over in an otherwise unused section of ground.

Until some giant trips and falls forehead first into it.

Mass times acceleration equals splat.

I watched his legs twitch in the grass, the hands that couldn't catch him shake in spasms.

Then I remembered he had a brother.

A brother with a big gun.

I hunched over and starting running again, working extra hard to ignore the pain in my hip, my ribs and between my legs.

It almost worked.

I heard the scream that rolled into a roar of agony.

When it stopped, I knew he was after me.

Part of it was the echo of shots sounding. I'm intuitive like that.

The other part was he told me.

"I'm coming for you!"

Like I was Murdoch and he was Rambo.

Big guys can't run long distance. That's the common thinking. Since I had been a marathon runner and longer in the past, I knew a thing or two about distance and pace.

There is a big difference between outrunning a lineman after ten miles and trying to get away in less than ten blocks.

Huge difference.

He had to be out of bullets, or maybe he just wanted to get closer for a better shot. Either way when I glanced behind me, he was gaining.

He carried a large sniper rifle that he must have looted from the National Guard armory. How they knew I was going this way I wished I could ask.

I always thought I was good at poker, but maybe I telegraph too many emotions on my face. Or talk in my sleep.

Or maybe Jean told them, I thought.

He was going to catch me.

The blows to my nether regions, the hits to the ground were taking their toll. I couldn't go full speed, and even half speed was a little faster than a tortoise.

We made JFK where it turned into main street, and I had a moment to think I skipped gangland when he reached me. Dumber swung the rifle like a bat, gripping the thick barrel in his giant hands.

I ducked just in time, close enough to feel the wind tug at the hair on the back of my head. I sent a rabbit punch into his kidney, a kick to his knee and hopped back to put ten feet between us.

He was not fazed. He pulled the gun back like a bat and twirled the end in the air as he stalked me.

"Got you," he grunted.

"Yeah, but how?" I thought I might as well ask as I danced back, working to keep the space between us.

"We been following you."

He swiped. I darted back and moved left. Dumber anticipated it and swung in the other direction. A switch hitter.

"Lost you in Sherwood. Then we heard you on the road."

He paced forward. I paced back. It wasn't a stalemate, just a delaying tactic. I was hurt and tired. He was hopped up on rage. I knew the feeling, tried to dig in and tap into my own.

It just wouldn't happen. My nuts hurt. My body hurt. I kept trying to think that he was the only thing between me and my kids, but it wasn't enough.

He was too close, the swings took too much concentration.

"You and your brother play baseball?" I asked.

Delaying tactic. Anything to throw him off.

He growled and swung again.

"Did you see him slide face first into home?"

A roar this time and he got close with the swing. His form was sloppy.

I backed up the street.

"Do you think he was safe? It was a close call, the ump said he was, but I think he's out. Forever."

I think he tried to say something.

Words were lost in spittle and screams as he charged. I did the duck and trip thing again.

It didn't work.

He dropped the rifle on my head and grabbed me by the ankle. Dumber did his best impression of an Olympic distance thrower, spinning me around in a circle and tossing me up the street.

It would have been a bronze medal throw. I blame my aerodynamics.

I hit the blacktop and rolled but didn't have time to get up.

Then he was on me. Like a Rhino on my chest. He tucked my chin against my chest, but he clubbed my head and jammed his massive hands around my throat.

Three minutes I thought, as the edge of my vision turned black. I had three minutes of air, give or take.

Except the blood flow to my brain was cut off too. I'd pass out in less than a minute.

I could see his face near mine, teeth locked in a grimace, lips curled in a snarl.

I didn't try to fight his hands. They were too big, too strong. I stabbed my thumbs into his open cheeks between teeth and

CHAPTER NINETEEN

skin and pulled. Cheeks are elastic and they stretch.

Only so far.

My grip was almost as strong as his, my arms bowed out and down. His skin split and sprayed blood across both of us.

He sat up and roared in pain and rage, raised both hands over his head to bring them down in a hammer blow to my face.

I had enough breath to realize this.

A Z latched on to his head.

Another grabbed him in a lumbering tackle and they folded back across my legs.

Zombies all around us, drawn by his screams, the sound of the gun, the noise of the fight.

He screamed as they bit him. I clawed my way free, felt one grip my coat. I shoulder checked it down, and crawled on hands and knees looking for free space.

I found it a few feet away and got up on shaky legs. My brain pounded in time with my racing heart as air rushed back into the starving cells. I'm glad my groin decided to take a break because Z poured into the street.

Most ignored me, drawn to the giant as he fought his way free and then went under another wave of the dead.

The ones who didn't ignore me shuffled in my direction.

I could stay ahead of them, but more were coming in from every direction. I limped toward downtown, dodging Z as I did, head on a swivel as I searched for someplace to hide, a roof to climb on, anything.

No weapon.

Too injured to run.

No time to make one.

Hiding was my only option, at least long enough to buy time and catch my breath.

They closed in, making the circle of grasping hands tighter, harder to dodge.

Then there was nowhere to go.

They were all around me.

One of the Z had a Deputies uniform on. His gun still in the holster.

I darted for him, used one hand to grip his shirt and hold his teeth away from me, fumbled with the other for the holster.

Glock 9, common enough for the police. I jammed it under his chin and pulled the trigger.

Nothing happened.

A Zombie grabbed my jacket and clawed for my neck, teeth chomping, the fetid stench of its breath covering me in a miasma.

Safety idiot.

I flipped off the safety, and blew a hole in the former gun owner's forehead, then turned it on the Z trying to eat me.

Fifteen shots in the magazine and it was full.

Fifteen Z fell around me, slow and steady.

I rooted around on the deputy's gun belt and found two additional magazines.

I'm not going to say it was a stroll in the park. I had forty-five shots and there were close to sixty zombies.

But the last twelve or so took a collapsible baton to the head, closer than I wanted to get, closer than reason dictated I should be.

In less than ten minutes I stood alone in the street, at the bottom of the overpass that ran over the railyard. Surrounded by dead zombies, splattered and sprayed with gore that dripped from the end of the baton onto the ground.

My nuts hurt.

CHAPTER NINETEEN

My ribs hurt.
My neck and head hurt.
I stank.
But I was alive.
I was David to two Goliath's.
And I had a pistol. No bullets.
Then I heard it.
"DAD!"

20

CHAPTER TWENTY

It was him. He was alive.

He was on top of the building next to the street and as I watched, he shimmied over the side and slid down the old drain pipe strapped to the wall with metal bands.

He dropped on the ground and ran toward me, hopping over dead bodies, cradling a hunting rifle strap to his chest.

He stopped five feet away and stared at me.

"What did you do?"

I opened my mouth to talk, but couldn't. The lump in my throat was too big. My eyes watered up and everything blurred.

"All of them?"

Was that wonder in his voice?

"I heard the big gun shooting," he said in a rush. "I got up here to watch, and saw you. I didn't know it was you or I would have helped."

He stepped closer then.

"I'm sorry Dad."

Sorry? Sorry for not helping me?

"Boy," I sobbed and grabbed him and wrapped my arms around him like I would never let go.

I felt his shoulders hitch as he cried too, head buried in my chest, a low sniffling snuffle of pain, and joy and suffering and release.

We held on like that for a long time.

When he pulled away, he smiled. I still couldn't get used to his thirteen-year-old face without braces, and he looked thin. Too thin. Worry lines around the edge of his hazel eyes. Hair longer than the last time I told him he was looking like a hippie.

My son.

"You look like shit, Dad."

Another thing I wouldn't get used to. The boy swearing. I guess I'd let a couple slide, it being the Z apocalypse and all, but he wasn't too old to take across my knee. Yet.

"You look like Mad Max."

He stepped back and indicated his outfit.

"The leather keeps the bite from going through."

"Good man," I said and secretly wondered why I thought layers instead of leather.

"What happened to you?" he asked and pointed to the scar line that ran along the side of my head.

"Someone shot me."

"They missed."

"It was close."

"Your face looks different too."

"Where's your sister?" I couldn't hold back.

I'd get the rest of the story later. What he had done to stay alive. But I had found one of my three and needed to know where the second was.

It was a hollow feeling in the pit of my stomach, an eternity of wondering between the time I got the question out and his face fell.

I wanted to sob again, but not in joy.

"I lost her," he started crying.

It was little boy tears, frustration and anger from letting me down. He was a man and he was supposed to protect his sister. That failure was eating him inside.

"When?"

"A week? Ten days," he blubbered.

I needed to get more details, and we needed to move. I could already see some Z wandering up the road, drawn by the noise and our presence.

"Come on," I grabbed his hand and started moving toward the Junction Bridge.

He dug in his heels and stopped me.

"We have to go back," he said. "That's where we said we'd meet."

CHAPTER TWENTY-ONE

He watched me build a small fire, and we sat in front of it, drinking water after it had boiled. If I had more time, we would have raided a few houses around us, but the Z massacre and fight had left me spent.

We were in the cafeteria that served as a gymnasium, nests of blankets on the floor for the two of them and a few others for kids they had met. No adults though, which surprised me.

A lot of orphans heading for school to hide out the zombie apocalypse.

"You look different Dad."

"I do?"

I bet I did.

But how do you tell your boy you've been shot? Blown up? Half drowned and ambushed? Chased? That you've killed more than zombies. Starved.

"Your hair is longer," he said.

Or skipped a haircut.

The boy had only known me with a buzz cut, my look du jour since I was nineteen. Easier to maintain, and let me focus on other more important things. I remembered a quote from John Malkovich who I wondered if he was a zombie now. He said upon losing his hair, "Good, now they can focus on the acting instead of how I look."

I felt that way about hair. Clothes. I wore the same type of thing to work every day, a sort of uniform for two reasons. I didn't care about fashion and I didn't want to waste time thinking about how to dress or what to wear.

Leave it to the boy to notice that.

"And someone tried to shoot you," he added.

And that too.

"They missed."

"Why was someone shooting you?" he poked at the embers with the end of a sharp stick.

"Which one?"

"There was more than one?"

"I've been asking myself that same question," I said.

He pointed to the side of his head where the scar was on mine.

Because I killed his men.

Because I took all this rage at your mom, and your stepmom but mostly at me and directed it outside.

Because they were trying to keep me from what I wanted and I'm the most selfish son of a bitch in the world.

"What did you do?"

He wasn't being serious. It was that same tone of voice he used to use when they came to visit or we stayed in the hotel, a mock accusation. It took me back to a dozen times when he had asked the same question in the same way, and we dissolved in laughter at whatever excuse I could manage to create on the spot.

God I loved this kid.

Zombies to the left of us, survivors all around and he still wanted to laugh with his dad.

My heart tripled in beat and I smiled through a shimmer of tears.

Everyone talks about the way a mother loves, but let me tell you a secret about a father's.

It's a love without end. Infinite.

It's guilt for missing and not being there, and guilt for still feeling that love. As if you don't deserve to feel that way.

I didn't have that with my dad. But somehow God smiled on me with my kids and I had it with them.

Not their mom's so much.

I cleared the lump in my throat and saw his eyes were shimmering too. The price of a zombie plague was my boy had to grow up too fast, and he relished this tiny moment. This connection.

"I took his milk money," I said. "I cut in front of him in line."

"In traffic," he smirked.

Even in the Z times, my hatred of traffic lived on in legend.

"He didn't use his blinker."

He snorted out a small giggle. Muted. Not anything like the giant guffaws, he once spewed. This was a trained way to laugh, something to keep the Z at bay, and a hiding place undiscovered.

"Tell me about your sister."

"We were out of food," he sniffed. "She took another kid that was here and they went hunting for it. But they never came back."

I breathed in, breathed out.

It was time to collect details.

There were a lot of Z I had seen in North Little Rock. She could be one of them. She could have been one of the ones I shot earlier.

"I told her I would wait for her."

"Did you know where she was going? Did you check there?"

He shrugged.

"We tried some houses around here, but there's still gangs. She was going to go up to the college and see if the cafeteria had food."

I had passed the road to the community college on my way down here. Literally two blocks from the place.

It was surrounded by tons of apartments, prime hunting ground to scavenge. Also, the potential for a ton of Z.

The fact that she hadn't come back in ten days left me feeling numb in my stomach, an ache worse than the ATV groin punch earlier.

But I also knew the key to survival was action.

"We'll go look at sunrise," I told him.

"I looked," he said again, ever the pragmatist.

"But this time you'll have two eyes."

That seemed to satisfy him and he curled up in his blanket. He didn't seem to mind that I started at him while he fell asleep. I nodded off after an hour of doing just that.

CHAPTER TWENTY-TWO

That night I dreamed of Brian, and wondered why it wasn't about Anna. I missed her. I suppose the dream was a way of telling me I missed him too, and now that I had one third of my family back, my brain was turning to the other survivors.

In the dream, he didn't speak to me, just sat by the fire we had built, and stared into the flames. There was no Peg, no Byron, no one but the two of us sitting across from each other in front of a fire.

When I woke, I was troubled.

A nagging sensation that I turned over in my mind, twisting the thoughts this way and that to see how they might fit together differently.

I had dreamed before the world was full of Z, and though I did not believe in fortune tellers or other less pragmatic things, I also once did not believe in zombies.

The reality of Z made me rethink my other preconceptions, and as some certain philosophers had pointed out in a dead free world, once you realize how much you don't know only then can you start learning.

I was open to the possibility that my brain was trying to tell me something, and the eerie feeling of dread the dream left me with lingered once the Boy woke up.

He rolled over and rubbed sleep from his still tired eyes and smiled at me.

"I wondered if I dreamed you," he said.

Then he scooted closer using his elbows and feet and curled up next to me, snuggled up against his dad and rested there.

I remembered reading that body language was ninety percent of communication and in that moment, my son was speaking a novel to me.

Glad I was there.

Glad I came.

Glad he wasn't alone.

"Me too," I told him.

"What?"

"I'm glad I'm here."

He nuzzled then, just twitching his arm and shoulders pressed against me. It lasted only a moment and not near long enough, and then he asserted his manliness by taking charge.

"We should go," he said.

I didn't want to go. I wanted him to sit back beside me, and I wanted Bem to walk through the door and settle in on the other side. And I wanted T to crawl up next to us, and we could stay there forever warm by the fire.

But my daughters were still out there.

There was no time to rest, no time to wait, and no time to

consider dreams or what they might mean.

There was only time to get moving. To find weapons, find food and find the girls.

"Guns," I told the Boy. "Food. Bem."

It was a simple checklist.

In the Z world, simple checklists were the best to follow.

The Boy stood up and wiped his hands on his leather pants.

"Okay Dad, where do we start."

CHAPTER TWENTY-THREE

The first thing we needed to do was get food. The cafeteria had been emptied out so it was into the surrounding neighborhood. Lucky for us their tiny little Catholic elementary school was in the middle of a lot of homes.

I told the Boy to be quiet and follow me, then led him down the sidewalk until we reached the River Trail. Little Rock created an attraction worthy of a much larger city when they installed the asphalt trail that ran seven miles along the river, crossed over at the Big Dam Bridge, and seven miles back up the other side. The trail was connected by three pedestrian bridges downtown to make one long loop.

When they first built it, I ran it every visit, which the kids hated and did not understand.

The Boy and I made our way along the trail past a rehab center to a new subdivision of riverfront mini-mansions. We checked doors and windows and broke in. The first had been cleared out.

We hit pay dirt on the second in the form of a full pantry. A couple of bangs on the doors inside proved we were alone, so we hunted for bags to carry the food.

The boy found a pretty princess backpack, and I didn't make him wear it after we had a can of soup each. Cold soup is not great, unless you're starving, in which case it tastes like ambrosia.

"Good," he smacked his lips and put the empty in the sink.

We searched the house, but couldn't find weapons. His gun was for show, the bullets long gone.

I knocked on the door to six other houses, but they were all fruitless searches. No more food. No guns.

I did find a hoe and rake in one garage, a rarity since these houses used a landscaper to do the yard work. I broke off the ends of each to make a five-foot sharp stake.

Perfect if we ran into a vampire. I guess it would work on the Z too.

Then we kept going up the River trail. I knew a shortcut that would lead us to the college on a mountain bike path that cut up the ridge from the north side next to Burns Park.

It took ten steps before I realized the Boy wasn't walking beside me. I stopped and shook my head. I was going to have to make sure I kept up with him, with all of them. He wasn't going to get out of my sight.

He stepped off the trail, stood next to a tree and began to pee.

"It's important to stay hydrated," I said to his back.

He turned his head halfway toward me and flopped to the ground like a puppet with the strings cut.

My stomach fell with him, my heart a microsecond behind as I listened for the echo of a gunshot. I willed my legs to move to him, to run but there was a short circuit in the wires. Voice didn't work. Legs didn't work.

"Don't move," a man stepped out of the woods behind me.

Camo insulated overalls made him look bigger than he was. The rifle I recognized, a .306, steady in his gloved hands, trigger finger cut out. He had a wool knit cap that covered his head, a scarf over his mouth. I could only see his wide eyes and the rifle that shot my son.

Something bubbled in my stomach.

He took a step toward me, gun aimed at my head.

"Dad!" the Boy shouted.

The gun swung toward his voice. I jumped forward as he jerked it toward me and tried to step back.

I got a forearm under the barrel and knocked it up. He squeezed the trigger and shot next to my ear. All I could hear was a ringing, and someone screaming.

By the time, I realized it was me, I knocked the hunter over like a turtle on his back and watched him struggle to roll over. I helped him flop to his stomach, grabbed the scarf and pulled until he stopped fighting, stopped moving.

I climbed off the body and turned around.

The Boy was standing ten feet away, scared eyes watching me. I took a step toward him and he stepped back.

"You killed him," he stuttered.

"I thought he shot you," I explained.

"I saw him moving," the Boy gulped. "I tried to hide."

"Don't do that," I stalked to him and wrapped him in a hug. "You're too good at playing dead."

He was stiff in my arms for a moment, still scared I guess, then relaxed into it.

"We've got to go," he whispered into my shoulder. "Z."

CHAPTER TWENTY-THREE

He pointed up the road. Z were streaming from the trees, drawn by the sound of the gunshot.

Maybe drawn by my screaming.

I bent down, grabbed the rifle and stripped a pack from the dead body before we rushed away from the Walking Dead.

CHAPTER TWENTY-FOUR

The hike through the woods was nice. The wind whispered through the leaves, the air was crisp but not cold, and my boy was behind me. I had a gnawing feeling in my stomach, but we finally had a gun that worked and food in a pack.

I had seen a couple of boats in the marina in front of the mini mansions that gave me an idea and if we didn't find Bem, we could bed down in one of them and search again tomorrow.

I wasn't sure how we were going to do a search pattern.

It would have been easier if we had cell phones. I'd just call her up and we could talk to each other until I found her.

Absent that I was going to set up a search pattern.

If the Boy knew which direction she had approached the school, we could have gone that way.

But they didn't coordinate like that.

It was a lesson learned.

CHAPTER TWENTY-FOUR

Once I had her back, we would always have a plan.

I took heart in the fact that the plan worked. Sometime in our past as we sat at dinner or in a hotel room in west Little Rock, I told them if something ever happened, leave me a note. I'll find you.

Who knows how that topic comes up.

I'm sure we were watching a TV show on the Disney channel that had zombies, and I said something off the cuff.

"Hey kids, if there's ever a Zombie Armageddon, write me a note and I'll come find you."

Except I did.

And they did.

Which means here we were.

Bem forgot to leave a note.

That didn't mean I couldn't find her. Just that it would take longer.

But it didn't.

It took long enough for us to walk past the Veteran's Home at Fort Roots perched on prime real estate above the River with an expansive view to the north and south.

We rounded a building that led to a quad across the street and a campus building beyond that.

There was a tower on the edge of the property, and a girl on the tower. Underneath her was a gang of men, boys really.

They sat waiting while she was tied to the tower so she wouldn't fall. I couldn't tell if she was sleeping or passed out.

"Back," I told the Boy and he ducked behind me.

Our movement so far hadn't attracted any attention and I did a head count. Eight boys under the tower, maybe more where I couldn't see. They all wore black head to toe, black tee shirts, black pants, black ball caps. I could see black metal glinting in their waistbands, pistols, but no one carried a rifle.

Five of them sat on the ground, backs leaning against the legs of the cell tower. Three catcalled up to her or roamed around underneath.

She was trapped.

"Do you know them?"

The Boy squinted around my shoulder.

"I think one is the brother of a kid that stayed with us a couple of nights. He got bit."

"Gang?"

"I think so."

Not everyone was swept up in the Zombie plague. Little Rock had one of the worst gang problems in the country and it was California's fault. A lot of people didn't think about what happened when criminals got a second strike.

The idea behind the Three Strikes law is if you're arrested and convicted of a crime three times, you're a habitual criminal and will go to jail for life. That's great for privatized prison industry, not so much for kids from the inner city who don't have a shot at a normal life. A lot of them hit their second strike before they were out of their teens.

Well-meaning parents or someone in their life decided to ship them off to a relative in Little Rock instead of San Quentin to save them from a life behind bars.

When the west coast gangs hit Mid-America, they brought the gang culture with them and descended on an unsuspecting populace. Drugs and violence followed in their wake as their numbers grew. Petty thugs who were low in the organization suddenly found themselves in fertile ground to become king-pins.

The gang wars started. It was bad enough that Little Rock

CHAPTER TWENTY-FOUR

made lists, all the while California was claiming a reduction in crime rates and a decrease in recidivism.

That's part of the problem with America. They don't solve problems, they just move them to a new location.

In Little Rock, good people abandoned the inner city to the gangs, which allowed them to run rampant.

It spilled over into North Little Rock and imitators popped up in the suburbs surrounding the cities, but Little Rock remained the epicenter.

Until the Z came.

I snickered.

"What?" the Boy asked.

"Gangs of Z are competing with the Bloods, Crips and whatever street Vice Lords now."

"That's not funny Dad."

"Not ha ha funny, but," I shrugged.

"You're weird. Maybe getting shot in the head affected your sense of humor."

My Boy, folks. He'll be here all week.

I glanced around the corner.

Eight of them.

I checked the magazine on the rifle. Six shots. I wasn't sure how long she had been up there, but I could see she strapped herself to a leg of the tower. There was an open backpack on her shoulders, and a couple of empty cans of food on the ground that could have been hers.

There was no time to wonder though.

Thugs had my girl trapped.

I don't know why. I didn't really care.

The familiar bubble of red gurgled in my stomach, and I let it wash up.

Six shots left five of them dead, the ones sitting by the tower. The other three scrambled for cover, shooting in the air in our general direction as they scattered.

"Stay here," I told the boy and ran with the rifle to the tower.

I frisked the pistols from the bodies around the base, and watched the perimeter, sticking one in the small of my back and two in the front.

"Bem!" I screamed and repeated her name again.

"Dad?" she sobbed.

I glanced up as she unbuckled the belt she was using as a strap, but her arms were too weak to hold herself up. She flipped over backwards and fell.

I dropped the rifle and caught her, just enough so we both went down to the ground. I cradled her in one arm and kept the pistol moving with the other, trying to watch our back, watch in all directions just in case any of her trappers came back.

"Can you walk?"

I hitched her up to carry her.

"My arms are asleep," she said in a daze. "I can walk."

She could, but barely. I think it was sheer willpower.

I'm glad she was hunched over because it gave us an excuse to duck as we shuffled back to the building.

The Boy grabbed her and hugged her close.

"It's Dad," she told him.

"I know," he assured her.

"I told you he would come."

"You doubted me?" I asked the Boy.

"There were a lot of zombies Dad. And people were trying to shoot you."

"We can wait here for them to come back and shoot me," I said. "Or we can move you someplace safe and get you food."

CHAPTER TWENTY-FOUR

She nodded in slow motion.

I lifted her up, held her in one arm and directed the Boy back to Fort Roots.

"Take us back to the trail."

CHAPTER TWENTY-FIVE

"I need to rest," she said and collapsed.

"How long were you up there?" the Boy kneeled beside her and held his water bottle to her lips.

"What day is it?"

"I don't know."

"Then more than three," she said. "Maybe five?"

"Is that why you smell like pee?"

"They wouldn't let me down to do it."

"What did they want?"

"Me."

"You."

"Me."

"Why?"

She gave him the look then, the one older sisters have been giving younger brothers since cave siblings walked upright.

"Oh."

There was a world of understanding in that statement.

We needed to scout ahead, but I wasn't going to let them out of my sight.

"Don't move," a voice called from behind us.

Damn it, we should have moved off trail.

I raised both hands in the air and slowly turned around.

The three men in black were advancing up the path, guns aimed at me. They ignored the kids, which was smart.

"You killed my brothers," said the lead guy.

I wasn't going to talk, not with guns aimed at my head. I needed to assess how stable they were, what they had planned, and not get shot. I didn't like getting shot.

"Get up," he told the kids.

They stood next to me on shaky legs, both holding on to me for support.

"Pull them guns out with your fingers," he told Bem. "You keep your hands up."

They hadn't shot me yet, which meant he had something worse planned.

Bem pulled the first pistol out and dropped it. She slowly moved her hand to the second gun and kept going to the ground, flopping on the dirt.

The three guns tracked her down and off me.

I felt the Boy rip the gun from the small of my back. He sent three quick shots their way, nailing two and sending the third spinning. I got the pistol out and up before he recovered and finished him off.

"Are you okay?"

Bem sat up.

"Dad, we planned it."

The Boy hustled to the fallen bodies and retrieved the pistols. He checked their pockets for bullets, but came up empty. Instead he held up a wad of cash folded into a rubber band roll.

"Why do you think they still carried cash?"

"Old habits die hard."

Bem picked up the gun she pulled from my waist and kept it. I took the three from the boy and stuck one in front, one in back and kept the last one out. It had a full magazine and the safety on.

We were armed.

We had a Princess backpack full of food.

And I had a plan.

CHAPTER TWENTY-SIX

We went back to the marina next to the giant brick tower, but I didn't want to take the boat on the water after dark.

The kids needed food and rest.

So did I.

Once we were floating downriver, we could find islands to camp on, and fish for food, but I knew of at least two dams we would need to negotiate, as well as the six bridges that spanned the river in just the city of Little Rock.

Plus, I wanted to catch up with the kids and get them both behind a fence so they felt safe, at least for the night.

We needed rest, some food, and some time with each other.

"We'll spend the night at your school," I told them. "And take the boat at first light."

I let the Boy lead the way back to the school and watched as he shimmied up the gutter to the open window, and slither inside.

He opened the locked door after a few seconds and I put him in charge of building a fire while I tried to clean up in what had once been the kitchen.

I could scrape the gray matter off, but the stains were set, so the jacket was a lost cause. I'd scrap it as soon as I could, but we would need all the layers we could get on the water.

When I walked back into the gym they made into a campground, the Boy had a small fire going and Em had two cans warming in the coals.

"I'm getting tired of beans," she used a pair of pliers to move a can in front of me, and the other in front of the Boy.

I spooned up a bite, then burned my fingers passing it back to her.

"We'll fish tomorrow. See if we can catch something fresh."

The promise of that seemed to satisfy her and she took a spoonful and passed the can back to me.

I made sure my bites were half sized, and that the boy ate all his. They noticed and appreciated it enough not to point it out.

"I wish I could have shot the second guy for you Dad."

I let him sit after dinner and wondered what he was thinking as we watched the fire die down. Emma curled up in a small ball and snoozed, the bottom of her feet against her brother's leg.

"You're fourteen son."

"Yeah, but when you were fourteen you told me you and uncle Doug were in the woods, building forts and booby traps and stuff."

What kind of parent tells their kid exactly what they did when they were fourteen? And more importantly, who knew the kid was listening!

He reminded me about my younger brother in California.

Doug and his family. Two kids and a wife. I wondered if he

was alive, if they made it. He had lived in a big city since he was twenty-five, and LA had thirteen million people around it. Fighting out of that many Z was almost impossible.

But then I had crossed half the country and fought a few Z and we both had the same training. Maybe my will was stronger, and I knew I was angrier. We're talking Hulk smash size anger.

He was way more mellow than me. Laid back. More friends, more people who liked him, including our parents and steps.

It wasn't that I was unlikeable.

A lot of people liked my company before the end of the world. I had a few close friends, could keep up a conversation with a stranger, and was a fine leader according to the people who worked with me and the surveys they took.

But I knew I was a stand-offish fellow.

I blame it on running by myself in the woods for hours on end.

That's a lot of time for self-reflection and discovery. Some people called it living in your head, some people called it discovering your center. Who knows who was right.

I know that after eighteen miles of exertion, the walls fall down and every emotion, every feeling is exposed. I ran without music which left me with the words in my head and song snippets stuck on loop.

I came up with a couple of philosophies, probably regurgitated from some first-year classes at University.

No one is right, this much I knew. Everything gets filtered through a point of view.

My memory of having fun in the woods could be my brother's nightmare of being dragged along doing something he hated. My feelings about my parents, even now thirty years later, could be wrong. Maybe they thought I was independent and nomadic and didn't want to be smothered.

All true things.

"Digging holes in the woods and fighting Z are not the same thing," I told him instead.

"I've been doing okay so far," there was a tinge of sulking in his voice.

It sounded a lot like me sometimes.

That made me smile, which made the set of his lips harder, and his eyebrows crinkle up. I snorted more.

"It's not funny."

"I know Boy. I know. And I'm so proud of you. You have no idea. I know how hard it's been. I know what you've had to do, what you're going to keep having to do. You made it. Your sister made it. That gives me hope."

"Hope for what Dad?" he pushed a branch further into the fire with the tip of his boot.

"We're going to find T. And I'm going to take you somewhere that we never had to fight a Z again."

"That's a pipe dream."

He was too young to be so cynical. But then maybe I had been too. The bane of having children is that for years they believe every word you say until a hormone dump makes them think everything is a lie.

It's why sixteen-year olds know everything, and just forget as they grow older.

I had been the same way. Part of that independence streak perhaps, or maybe the Boy got it from me, encoded in his DNA.

"It's a promise."

We sat and stared at the fire in silence, the crackle of the wood and pops of sap in the pine back the only sounds.

"I'm going to check the perimeter," I stood up.

Bem stirred, but the Boy reached over and patted her leg and she drifted back to sleep.

"You should sleep too. We're moving out at sunrise."

He nodded and shifted down to the floor, careful that he didn't disturb his sister. I watched him close his eyes and felt another wave of sadness.

It reminded me of something I had read a long time ago.

A soldier grabs sleep when he can, and learns to sleep anywhere. The Boy was a solider now in the Z war. I'd learn about what they had done to survive, because I had a million questions. I could ask when we were on the water and it would help the miles go by faster.

But I'd never tell them what I did, what I'd done.

The Boy had seen some of it, and it changed the way he looked at me.

I didn't like it.

The door was secured shut, and I walked around to peer through the windows.

I glanced at the fence that surrounded the property, the view slightly distorted by the mismatched diamond patterns of the chain link outside and the security window stripes.

The Z stood against the fence, unmoving, staring at us, or maybe the orange glow that flickered through the window.

They didn't moan, they didn't shove, just stood in line and watched.

It was a weird feeling that made chills do a dance up and down my spine.

One of the Z looked like Jean.

THE END

ABOUT THE AUTHOR:

Chris Lowry is an avid adventurer and ultrarunning author. He divides his time between Florida, Arkansas and California where he trains for 100 mile Ultramarathons. He has completed over 68 races, including 18 marathon's and 12 Ultramarathons and is planning a Transcontinental Run across the United States from Los Angeles to New York City in 2017. He has kayaked the Mississippi River solo, and biked across the state of Florida. When not outdoors, he is producing and directing a documentary film about adventure and writing. His novels include the Battlefield Z series, the Marshal of Magic Series and the Shadowboxer Files. He loves good craft beer and meeting with reading clubs and running clubs, especially if the aforementioned beer is offered.

ABOUT THE AUTHOR:

Have you joined the adventure?

Battlefield Z

Battlefield Z – Children's Brigade

Battlefield Z – Sweet Home Zombie

Battlefield Z – Zombie Blues Highway

Battlefield Z – Mardi Gras Zombie

Battlefield Z – Bluegrass Zombie

Battlefield Z – Outcast Zombie

Battlefield Z - Renegade Zombie

Battlefield Z - Everglades Zombie

More adventures in the series

FLYOVER ZOMBIE – a Battlefield Z series

HEADSHOTS – a Battlefield Z series

www.ingramcontent.com/pod-product-compliance
Lightning Source LLC
LaVergne TN
LVHW041708060526
838201LV00043B/627